The Trave

Written b
Cover De..._
Illustrations: Tara Faul
Editor: SJS Editorial Services

Published by Nicholas Goss, Nashville, TN
Copyright © 2019 Nicholas Goss

Publisher's Note: This is a work of fiction. Names,
characters, places, and incidents are a product of
the author's imagination. Locales and public names
are sometimes used for atmospheric
purposes. Any resemblance to actual people, living
or dead, or to business, companies, events,
institutions, or locales is completely coincidental.

Printed in the United States of America
ISBN 978-1-7321815-6-4 (Paperback)

Note from the Author

Dear Reader,

I hope you enjoy reading this book as much as I enjoyed creating the story within it. The next story in this series is even better because of the feedback I receive from parents and children.

I highly value any and all feedback about my story, the writing, editing, artwork, etc. If you would please leave an honest review of this book, on the site from which you purchased it, it will help others make a more informed buying decision.

With all of my heart, thank you for purchasing this book! Now let's continue the adventure...

~ Nick

Dedication

For my son.

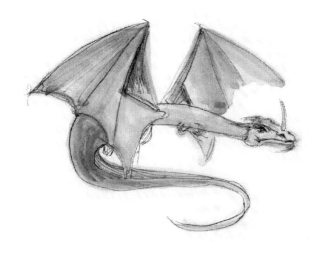

Fire & Chaos

The Traveler's League - Book 3

By Nick Goss

Table of Contents

"In Traveler's Rest you'll find friends."

-*The Traveler's Code, Article XII.*

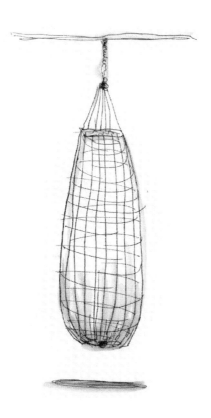

Fox in the Henhouse

"Tell me again, why are we doing this?" Christian was getting tired of all the physical labor. He had spent hours moving wooden benches, boxes, and tables from one wall of the Traveler's Rest to another.

Eli reminded him of the plan, "If we rearrange everything in the clubhouse, the fox will be easier to catch. And if he appears when we're away, or asleep, he'll be disoriented enough to fall into my trap."

"You mean *GeriPog's* trap?" Christian corrected Eli. GeriPog was the master of setting traps and snares. When he served Braxo, he was the only one clever enough to entrap a traveler. His lure and springing net in the WolliPog village was pure genius. Eli had complimented GeriPog several times on his accomplishment. Travelers are smart, fast, and much bigger than the average WolliPog.

"Yeah. I guess I should give credit to the dwarf. This was his idea." Eli paused for a moment and smiled at Christian sarcastically. "So you can complain to him. I'm sure he'll understand."

GeriPog didn't like to hear the boys complain. He'd just as well slap a boy for complaining than listen to him make excuses. He had originally planned to go with Toby to find this 'fox' kid. But after the battle in the chamber, he felt keeping Eva Mae in Traveler's Rest was the safer, more prudent course. That meant waiting around, surrounded by a bunch of whiny boys.

"I think I'll just keep helping you move stuff and avoid getting dwarf-slapped." Christian and Eli laughed together.

An hour later, they were finished. The tables and benches had been rearranged, laid out in the middle of the room in a strange pattern with no symmetry or reason. The raised platform where Travelers magically arrived, was moved from the north wall to the west wall. The big, yellow curtain that covered the portal to the Chamber of Crossroads, was moved from the south wall to the east. It was important that the curtain and the platform be directly opposite of each other. The glowing portal embedded in the south wall was then blocked from view by the dozens of wooden crates, boxes, and storage lockers that Eli stocked and organized. He was the Keeper, in charge of all the supplies and provisions for the Traveler's League. He was also a 'Club Knight,' part of the special group that volunteered to stay at Traveler's Rest, guard Eva Mae and the clubhouse, and capture Smitty the fox. Christian was the leader of the Club Knights. About thirty boys volunteered to guard Traveler's Rest with him. The rest of the boys, the Fox Hunters, went off with Toby to search the five worlds for Smitty the fox, capture him, and take back the timepiece he had stolen.

With the clubhouse sufficiently rearranged, GeriPog began the work of building his snare. He didn't tell anybody exactly what he was doing and would allow no boy to help him. In fact, he didn't want any of the boys to get close enough to see the details of his craft.

"If I can smell your breath, you're too close!" he grumbled at one boy who looked over his shoulder. "And I can smell a rabbit fart from a mile away."

Another boy offered to help GeriPog build the trap. The old dwarf sarcastically said, "Sure! That'd be great. I need to test it on someone unimportant... just in case it doesn't work, and we lose a boy." That boy politely decided to help Eli count supplies instead.

The old dwarf had turned good but was still grumpy. Just because he no longer served Braxo the black wizard didn't mean he wasn't a sour old WolliPog. The only person who softened him was Eva Mae. When she was around, he spoke gently to her like a loving grandfather, or like a lonely old man who brings home a lost puppy. Eva Mae was his friend, his master, and his queen.

"It's done," GeriPog said to nobody and everybody. "Don't nobody get close to this curtain. You'll spring the trap and be in for the surprise of your life."

Christian jumped up on the platform. "You all know what to do. We'll take shifts going into the chamber on patrol. Two at a time. Always go in with a buddy. If there's trouble, one comes back for help. The rest of us will stay here and sleep. We'll rotate patrols every two hours. Eli, please keep track of time. I'll go on patrol first." Christian got a volunteer to go with him and they disappeared into the portal.

Eli looked at his watch and said, "We should get some sleep, guys. I'll wake you one at a time when it's your turn to go into the chamber." One by one, the boys stretched out on the tables, benches, and spots on the floor. They had no problem falling asleep on the wooden surfaces as Eli passed out blankets and a pillow for each boy. Eva Mae got two blankets and two pillows. She didn't ask for them, but GeriPog made sure Eli treated her with extra consideration.

Soon, the whole clubhouse was quiet. The only sounds heard were the heavy sleepy breaths of thirty boys drifting off to dreamland. When Eva Mae fell asleep, GeriPog sat on top of a crate with his legs crossed, in a dark corner that gave him visibility to the whole room, especially the curtain. In his hand was a small cord. He called it 'the trigger rope.'

An hour went by, but nothing happened. Then two hours passed. Christian and his fellow patrolman re-emerged from behind the boxes that hid the portal. They whispered with Eli, who tiptoed into the room to wake up two boys for the next patrol in the Chamber of Crossroads. Christian found a nice spot at the foot of the platform near GeriPog's corner and quickly fell asleep.

Not a single noise was heard It had been about three hours. Only the dark eyes of the dwarf were open as he watched over Eva Mae and the Club Knights. Suddenly, a soft sound, like the rustling of air, wisped through the clubhouse.

Whoosh.

A tall shadow appeared on the platform. It was taller than most of the boys, but not quite as tall as a grown man. The shadow remained perfectly still, moving only its head from side to side, trying to see into the dark-lit clubhouse. His eyes must be adjusting. *That's why he's not movin' yet*, thought GeriPog. A few moments later, the thin shadow softly stepped down from the platform and moved across the room. The single candle on the wall by the curtain gave just enough light to reveal the red hair of a teenage boy. *The fox returns to the henhouse.* GeriPog was certain it was

Smitty. He gripped the trigger rope tightly and waited for the right moment.

The fox stepped ever so carefully over a sleeping boy on the floor in front of the curtain, then reached out to grab the yellow fabric. He slipped one arm behind the curtain, then a leg. He slowly slid with his back against the wall behind the yellow fabric. GeriPog waited until the fox was *completely* behind the curtain, then yanked the rope with a sharp tug.

Twang!

Three loops that had been laying on the floor sprang up, noosing Smitty's legs. A large wooden table that had been propped upright against the north wall fell over with a *bang*! And the weight of the table was enough to pull Smitty into the air by his feet.

The bang of the table woke every boy. When they jumped up and wiped the sleep from their eyes, they saw Smitty the fox hanging from the ceiling, upside down. He was growling and shouting curse words. The boys' faces turned red when they heard the dirty words that came out of their former captain's mouth.

GeriPog stood under the dangling redhead. He bent over and picked up the timepiece off the wooden floor and slipped it in his pocket. Smitty had dropped it when he was yanked off his feet and into the air by GeriPog's fox snare.

"You should really take better care to hold onto this pretty watch, boy." The dwarf chuckled.

Christian walked up to Smitty and coldly stared at him. Without looking away, he yelled back over his shoulder, "Hey, Eli! You want to take a swing at the fox piñata?"

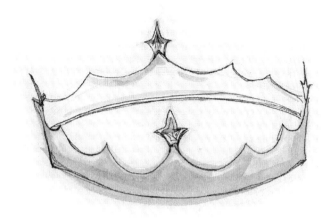

The Five O'clock Queen

Few boys slept well that night. It was hard to fall asleep with the excitement of capturing Smitty pulsing through the clubhouse. And it was hard to sleep when the red-headed teenager shouted dirty words at everyone. GeriPog did his best to silence Smitty so the rest of the boys could sleep, but gags and face slaps didn't seem to work.

Toby arrived the next morning with the Fox Hunters. One by one, they emerged from behind the pile of crates and boxes. The last of the boys to appear was Hoops. Smitty writhed and squirmed in fury when he saw him. He never hated anyone as much as Hoops.

Christian proudly boasted, "Welcome back, Cap. While you were away, we had the distinct honor of capturing the fox. As you can see, the rearranged room, coupled with the genius of GeriPog's snare, worked like a charm."

"Great job, Christian! Is everyone okay? Did anyone get hurt?" Toby asked.

GeriPog answered for Christian, "The fox got his pride hurt, no doubt. But no, no one was harmed."

Christian stepped towards Smitty and said, "Aw... did the widdle foxy woxy get his widdle fee-wings hurt?"

Smitty wriggled in mid-air and spewed curses through his gag while Christian and GeriPog laughed.

Toby stared coldly at Smitty. Without taking his eyes off him, he shouted back over his shoulder, "Hey, Eli. Would you like to take a couple of swings? You have the right to take revenge, and it won't bother me one bit to see you give Smitty a bloody nose."

Eli walked up to Smitty and grabbed his red hair with his left hand and raised his right arm. His hand was balled up in a fist. The room was silent. Justice was about to be served and every boy held his breath. Eli glanced around the room at the faces of his friends, the boys he'd served for so long. *What am I doing? Is this the kind of thing a traveler should do? These boys look up to me.*

"Nah. He's not worth it to me. Besides, what would Dewin say if he were here? This isn't something that would make our old friend proud."

Christian said, "Eli, you're an awesome guy! I would have smacked the red hair right off his pouty little face, only to regret it later on. You're right. Dewin wouldn't approve of this."

Toby chimed in, "I'm a little embarrassed I even suggested it, guys. Not very leader-like, I guess. Thanks for doing the right thing, Eli."

GeriPog echoed Toby, "Yes, thanks for doing the right thing, Eli. Please allow me..." The dwarf spun around and slapped Smitty in the face so hard his whole body swayed back and forth like a pendulum. Nobody cheered. It seemed in bad taste that GeriPog would strike a captured enemy now that he was a good guy. But GeriPog wasn't a member of the Traveler's League. He wasn't held to their rules, standards, or principles. He was his own dwarf and lived by his own rules.

Toby asked where the timepiece was.

"I've got it here." GeriPog patted his pocket with his chubby little hand. "And I'll be giving it to the girl. It belongs to *her*."

"The timepiece belongs to the Traveler's League," Toby corrected the dwarf. "And I, for one, agree that she should have it. But I would like Eli to examine the watch to make sure it's in good condition."

"Fair enough." GeriPog motioned for Eli and they sat at a table together. The dwarf handed over the watch and folded his arms. He watched the Keeper like a hawk. Eli took his time, looked over every detail, then handed it back. GeriPog grabbed it like a spoiled child and waddled over to Eva Mae. Everything about him changed when he spoke to her. He knelt in front of her on one knee and held the timepiece out before him.

"I believe this belongs to you, my lady. I stole it from you, cruelly, many weeks ago. Please forgive me."

"You're my best friend, GeriPog. Best friends forgive each other always," Eva Mae chirped. "But I don't want the watch anymore. I don't want to travel."

The room fell silent again, and several boys gasped. Christian gasped so hard, he fainted and fell over on his side, still awake.

"But the watch... chose you," Hoops interrupted. "You can't just stop traveling."

"She can do what she wants, boy!" GeriPog barked at him, still on one knee.

Christian threw his hands up in the air. "Well? Isn't this just great? We've gone through all this work, all this planning, to get the watch back to Eva Mae. And she doesn't even want it! She can't be a member of the Traveler's League if she doesn't finish her travels." The boys around the room all agreed with Christian. He turned towards Eva Mae and continued, "We can't vote you into the League until you do. I'm sorry. I think you're great. Everyone here really likes you. You'd probably be voted in with no problems. But we've all earned the *right* to be members by completing our travels."

"That's okay," Eva Mae said softly. "I don't really want to be a member."

"You what...?" Every boy gasped at once.

Toby stepped next to GeriPog. "Eva Mae, are you saying that you want me to take you home? Back to the six thirty? If I do, I'll have to give the watch to someone else."

"I don't want to go back to the six thirty. I want to go back to Sirihbaz."

The room was dead quiet. Toby shifted. "I'm confused. We worked really hard to free you from Sirihbaz, from the dungeon."

"No. You worked really hard to rescue me from *Braxo*. Now that he's dead, I want his castle. I killed him, so I get all his stuff. Isn't that right, GeriPog?"

The dwarf wrung his hands together and a big grin split his scarred face. "That's exactly right, my queen."

"Queen?" Christian asked. "Where did *that* come from?"

"From ME!" GeriPog grunted. "I'll escort her back to Castle Mavros and care for her every need."

"Together, we can rebuild the village. I want to free the WolliPog, too, and make Sirihbaz beautiful again." Eva Mae looked at the concerned faces of the boys around her. They all had families, friends, and people who expected them to return home to the six thirty. They had people who loved them and would worry about them if they didn't return. "I'm an orphan. My parents died a couple of years ago in a car crash. I want to stay with GeriPog. He's my family now."

She held out the timepiece towards Toby. "What do you say, Captain? Can I stay in Sirihbaz?"

"Sure." Toby gently took the pocket watch. "Just make sure that when a traveler comes through the five o'clock world, they are taken care of. With Dewin gone, they'll need every friend they can get."

Eva Mae took GeriPog's hand and looked Toby directly in the eyes. "I promise that Sirihbaz will be a safe place for the Traveler's League." With that, she disappeared behind the boxes and crates that covered the portal to the Chamber of Crossroads. The Five O'clock Queen was returning home.

Smitty is Banished

Toby ordered that Smitty's arms and legs be tied before cutting him down from the snare. Smitty hit the ground with a loud *thump* and wriggled himself up onto his feet. He hopped to a bench nearby and sat.

"Water, Eli," Toby ordered. The Keeper handed a canteen to Toby who placed the open lid up to Smitty's mouth. Smitty took a long draw and filled his cheeks. For a brief moment, Toby turned his head and winced, expecting Smitty to spew the water all over him. But Smitty swallowed and took a deep breath.

"I don't care what happened, or why you left. I'm not interested in hearing about how you were done wrong, or something was unfair. All I want to know is *why* did you return to Traveler's Rest?" Toby had practiced what he'd say when he saw Smitty face to face. Now the moment had come.

Smitty shifted to get a little more comfortable. "I was just trying to help my friends."

"You don't have any friends here." Toby's voice was ice cold.

"Yeah. I figured that was the case." Smitty wouldn't look Toby in the eye. "But I was talking about my *new* friends. My true friends... They needed some help. They're stuck, you see. They're stuck in a bad place and need me to get them out. I can only do that from the chamber. I was just trying to get into the chamber. I was going to leave the timepiece with the League and just use the portals once I helped my new friends. My true friends."

None of this made sense to Toby. He wondered if Smitty had somehow sided with Braxo but didn't know that he was defeated. "Braxo is dead, Smitty. We beat him. We beat him and his whole WolliPog army."

"Poor old Braxo," Smitty pretended to feel pity. "The Four Gates and Five Worlds are safe again. I'm glad he's no longer a threat."

Toby was getting irritated. "Is he the friend you were trying to help?"

Smitty snickered. "Uh, no. Why would I be friends with that sadistic, evil buffoon?"

"Well, who are these new friends you're talking about?" Toby demanded.

"My new friends? They're my *true* friends." Smitty toyed with him. They sat in silence for a few minutes. Toby glared at the fox, wondering how he could have gone off the rails. Smitty seemed different now. When he was hanging upside down, he cursed and shouted and struggled. But when Toby sat him down and talked with him, he seemed distracted, daydreamy, and docile. Smitty didn't make any sense when he talked either. He just rambled on and on about 'new friends, true friends.'

"That's it." Toby gave up trying to get answers and threw his hands up in the air. "I'm taking you home." He grabbed the ropes around Smitty's hands and pulled him to his feet. Toby led him over to the platform and pulled the timepiece from his pocket.

"Eli, I'll be back in a few minutes."

"Be careful, Toby. He's dangerous..." Eli watched as Toby set the timepiece for six thirty and rubbed. As the whirl of magic dust encircled Toby, he placed his hand on Smitty the fox's shoulder. They both vanished from sight.

Whoosh.

They appeared in a city park, behind a small grove of trees near a fountain. Smitty looked around and snickered.

"What's so funny?" Toby grunted.

"Oh nothing, just brings back memories... Toby, are you going to cut me loose? These ropes are really tight. I can't do anything but hop around. And what if I need to go to the bathroom?"

Toby said, "Not my problem."

"What happens when an adult sees me come out from behind these trees all tied up? I'll tell them that a teenager with black hair covering half of his face robbed me!" Smitty was getting red from anger.

"Tell them whatever you want." Toby began to rub the watch.

"I'm going to tell the police I was kidnapped! And that YOU, Tobias Middleton Sharp, were the mastermind behind it. You'll never be able to show your face in the six thirty again!" Smitty was practically shouting in anger, but Toby had already vanished. Surely, he had heard most of Smitty's railing.

I'm going to get that watch back, and I'm going to make your life miserable if you ever try to come home, Toby.

Smitty hopped out from behind the trees and did exactly what he promised he'd do. He cried for help. He worked up some fake tears and told some nearby adults that a big, black-haired bully had kidnapped him. When he got home, he told his parents the same story. When his parents called the police, he told them Tobias Middleton Sharp kidnapped him, robbed him, and left him tied up behind some trees in the park.

Wanted posters went up all over the city with Toby's face on them. Smitty made sure every teacher, librarian, police officer, mailman, garbage man, and taxi driver knew who Tobias Middleton Sharp was and what he looked like. Smitty spread his lies all over town. Toby had become a monster to everyone that knew him in his home world.

Toby arrived back at Traveler's Rest alone. When he stepped off the platform, Eli set his journals and checklists down and ran over.

"How did it go? Are you okay? Did he make trouble?"

"It went as well as it could have, I guess. I left him in the park, tied up. He was pretty mad." Toby was worried. Just before he had vanished, he heard Smitty's threat about going to the police. He knew that Smitty was already causing problems for him and the Traveler's League back home. He didn't say anything about the police to Eli, though. "I need to get the timepiece to the next traveler as soon as possible. We could use more members. After the battle, I heard a lot of the newer guys complaining about wanting to go home. And a few of them felt sorry for the fox. I'm sure Smitty will be working against us in the six thirty, convincing kids we're dangerous kidnappers, bullies, blah, blah, blah... Anyway, we need more members of the League. I think tough times are ahead."

Toby gathered all the boys around the platform and stood to address them.

"I know things have been exciting over the past couple of days. You guys have been awesome. You've been courageous, loyal, and helpful. We defeated Braxo and captured the fox!" The boys shouted and clapped and cheered for a moment, then Toby continued, "Smitty violated our trust as captain, assaulted one of our own and stole the timepiece. As the new captain of the Traveler's League, I hereby banish him from membership, from Traveler's Rest, and from the Four Gates and Five Worlds." The boys were silent. Toby continued, "You need to know that Smitty is working against us. He's stuck in the six thirty now, and he's spreading lies about us. You can expect trouble from your parents and teachers when you return home. Now that Braxo is gone and the five worlds are at rest, I think you should all go back to the six thirty until things settle down there. I'll have to stay here to keep an eye on things. I'm also going to give the timepiece to the next traveler. I'll summon you all again when the new kid makes it through the worlds. In the meantime, do everything you can to fight the fox's lies at home. You are now *at ease, Travelers.*"

The order 'at ease' triggered the ancient magic that powered the gold medals dangling from each traveler's shirt. One by one, the boys vanished, whisked back to their homes in the six thirty. Within seconds, Toby was alone in Traveler's Rest. Even Eli had been sent back home. The clubhouse seemed more than just quiet. It seemed darker without any of his friends. So much had happened over the past couple of days, the sudden emptiness and quietness made Toby feel more than just alone, he felt lonely.

He popped the lid of the timepiece open and set it for twelve o'clock. Just for good measure, he wound it up nice and tight, then snapped the lid shut. A quick brush of his thumb over the lid was enough to set the magic to work. The wooden tables, benches, boxes, and crates disappeared as the tornado of electric dust particles snatched Toby away to find the next traveler.

Whoosh.

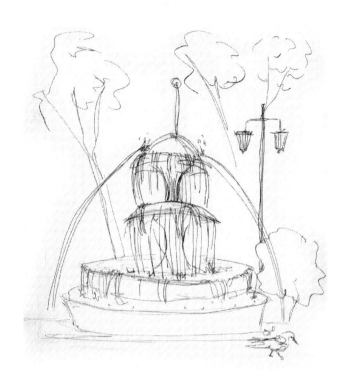

Cops and Robbers

"Stop right there!" the policeman yelled. He grabbed at his radio transmitter on his shoulder as he began to chase. "Officer Sanchez to dispatch, calling in a 10-80, over." Toby could hear the squeak of the police radio behind him over the heavy footsteps of the officer's feet pounding against the sidewalk. "In pursuit of suspect Tobias Sharp…"

Toby ran for his life. He had feared that Smitty was telling the truth. The fox had threatened to spread lies about being kidnapped by Toby. But the new captain of the Traveler's League hoped that Smitty had been simply making threats. It was clear that Smitty had taken the step and became a conniving, deceitful enemy.

"I'm in Grandville Park. Suspect is on foot, heading north towards Chestnut Street…" Even though Officer Sanchez was a little chubby, he was quick on his feet. He could get within twenty feet of Toby but no closer. "I'm going to need backup, over."

Backup? Dang it! I'm toast. Toby ran like a rabbit being chased by a wolf. One wrong step and he would find himself in the jaws of the predator. He couldn't get caught. There was too much at stake. If he was arrested, they would take the timepiece away from him. He couldn't find the next traveler and would have no way of getting back to Traveler's Rest. The six thirty world, like all the others, had a hidden portal that led directly into the Chamber of Crossroads, but Toby had never used it and didn't know where it could possibly be. As the Retriever, he had used the secret portals to enter and exit every world. But never once did the need arise for him to secretly travel back home.

The officer was getting winded and fell behind quite a bit. Toby felt fear pumping through his body and was unaware of how hard and fast his own legs carried him. The blood rushed through his ears as he looked down the path ahead. Just past the playground, he could see the big fountain that marked the middle of the Grandville Park. And surrounding the fountain were thick groves of maple trees and hedges, perfectly manicured to form a circular wall around the beautiful feature of the park.

Behind him, Toby heard the police radio squeak again, "...copy that, Sanchez... *calling all units, 10-80... officer needs assistance. In pursuit of kidnapping suspect Tobias Sharp in Grandville Park. Suspect is heading north towards Chestnut. Please respond, all units...*" The center of the park was only a few yards ahead and Toby headed for the thick bushes on the other side of the fountain and dove into them head first. He scrambled on his hands to where the hedges were the thickest and hid himself behind the trunk of a large tree. The officer had stopped at the edge of the bushes briefly, then began to slowly and loudly push his way into the thick shrubbery.

"It's no use, Toby. Come out now and talk to me. You can't get away. You can't live your life on the run. You need to own up to what you've done, kid. The more you run, the worse you're going to make things."

Toby's heart beat like thunder in his chest, and as he struggled to catch his breath, he heard the whiny sirens of several police cars in the distance. *They're coming for me! I can't believe this is happening. My parents. Oh no. They're going to kill me! What have I done? I've got to get out of here.*

Sanchez was close. It was now or never. Toby pulled the timepiece from his pocket and set it for eleven o'clock.

"He's over here! Officer! Toby's over here!" Smitty's voice came from a few yards away. The redhead was up in a tree. When the commotion began, he had climbed up to watch for Toby and help the police. He had been waiting in the park for this moment. Every day since he returned, he hung out in the park, knowing that the captain of the League would eventually show up and try to pass on the timepiece. Today was the day he would get revenge. He scrambled up the tree when he heard police sirens and spotted Toby crawling through the bushes and, from the look on his face, he enjoyed the show.

As soon as Toby realized it was Smitty's voice coming from the branches above, a rough hand reached around the tree and grabbed his arm.

"Gotcha!" Officer Sanchez easily held Toby down on the ground and swiftly handcuffed his hands behind his back. The timepiece fell to the ground and Sanchez picked it up and slipped it into his pants pocket.

Toby was pulled to his feet. Hanging his head in shame, he tried to hold back the tears.

Smitty jumped down from his nearby tree as Officer Sanchez led Toby out from the bushes and towards the fountain.

"Wait! Officer..."

The policeman turned towards the redhead and said, "Not now, kid. I need you to stay back."

"But he stole my pocket watch! I just want my pocket watch back."

Sanchez reached in his pocket and pulled out the timepiece. He held it in his hand as he grabbed at his radio on his shoulder. "Suspect in custody. We're at the fountain in the center of the park, over." As he waited for dispatch to respond, he looked at the red-headed teenager and tossed the pocket watch to him.

"Thank you, officer," Smitty said while he smiled like a devil at Toby. But Officer Sanchez wasn't paying attention and as the police dispatch responded over the radio, the fox slipped back into the bushes.

A moment later, as Toby and the officer waited by the fountain for the other police to arrive, Toby heard a sound that only a traveler would recognize coming from behind the hedges.

Whoosh.

The Old Town Boys

A mile south of Grandville Park, there was a border. It wasn't a border between countries, or an uncrossable border. It was a set of rusty old train tracks that wound down from the hill country in the east and stretched out in a straight line to the barren west. There hadn't been a train on those tracks in years, decades even. The city had outgrown the need for trains. It had a web of freeways that connected it to all the other major cities on the coast and in the mountains. It had a regional airport, taxis, and buses for public transportation, but rail cars were a thing of the past.

There was a time when the city was just a town, a lonely outpost between the big coastal cities, and the wild, unsettled plains and deserts to the west. Train tracks led the way to new opportunities and adventures for families who wanted a new start at a better future. Grandville thrived as trains stopped for supplies and spilled their passengers out for a break from the hours-long trek from their last stop. It was a community that grew as more families arrived and settled at this new waypoint. Houses were built on both sides of the tracks. The "Old Town" was the section to the south of the tracks. It was the beating heart of commerce and settlement for decades. But as the wealthier passengers arrived on trains, they wanted to build their homes to the north of the tracks, where they could keep to their own kind, build big houses, and put their money into city projects that catered to the richer folks.

Eventually, the freeways and airports came along, and the passenger trains disappeared. Old Town became a rundown, dirty part of the city, where the crime was high, and the people were low, and poor. The sidewalks crumbled, and weeds grew everywhere. The families that didn't have the money to live north of the old tracks in the "New Town" had to live in tiny homes packed tightly together.

Thanks to the rich folks, all of the city's schools were built north of the tracks. Poor and rich kids alike attended school side by side. The biggest school was on the edge of Grandville Park.

Smitty grew up in Old Town. He walked a mile to school every day and spent all of his free time at Grandville Park. He loved school and the park because they were in a clean and safe part of the city. He hated crossing the border into Old Town, where the bullies and crooks lived. He hated the dirt and weeds and broken-down buildings. He hated the old, empty stores and barbed-wire fences. He hated the smell of the sewer and the noise of police sirens. But most of all, he hated walking home. He grew up being warned of the danger of bullies and strangers, and he always made it a point to walk home with a group of other kids from Old Town. His two best friends, Spencer and Buck, had grown up making the daily, mile-long walk with him. They were poor just like Smitty.

Spencer and Buck were identical twins. They both had long, uncut, dirty-brown hair. They rarely bathed because sometimes the water in their tiny, filthy home didn't run. And there were many days that they didn't eat at home because their parents didn't have enough money to buy food. On these days, they would only eat at school, because lunch was free. It didn't take long for Spencer and Buck to figure out that they could bully other kids at school and steal their lunch. Smitty didn't like that his best friends were the school bullies but having two big, dumb brutes at his side at certain times had been useful. So, he always stuck up for them, and he always stayed close to them. But he was ten times more clever than the twins and had gotten them out of trouble on several occasions.

They're perfect.

Smitty sat by the fire blazing at the entrance of the cave. The heavy darkness of the shadow world concealed an unknown realm full of mystery around him. He stared into the flames as the cold, airy whispers grew louder in each ear. His new friends, his *true* friends, kept sharing secrets, stories, and... promises. They were trapped in shadow, but Smitty could help free them. And in exchange for their freedom, they would give him what he always wanted. They would make him rich... and powerful. They would reveal the magic of the five worlds and teach him all of the ancient secrets of Sirihbaz, Torpil, Animas, and Hapis. If they could only be released, they would teach him, and serve him.

Releasing his new friends from the shadows would require him to find two boys with strong bodies and weak minds.

"Bring them to us..." the cold wind in his left ear instructed.

"Into the chamber..." the icy breath said in his right ear.

Then both voices in unison chanted, *"...and we will be freed."*

"And then what?" Smitty asked again. He had asked that question a dozen times already and the answer remained the same: *"We will restore the wonders of Skuggi, and you will rule the Four Gates and Five Worlds."*

Shadows in the Chamber

"What just happened?" Spencer was wide eyed, and his mouth hung open. "Where are we?"

Buck just stood there staring into the darkness of the clubhouse. No words could come out of his big, dumb mouth. He was in shock. Both boys trembled. Smitty didn't tell them what would happen. He had only told them to grab his arms and close their eyes as he rubbed the timepiece.

"There is this club of wimpy kids. Nerds, mostly. They call themselves *the Traveler's League*. And this place is their clubhouse. They meet here occasionally and brag about their adventures and pretend to be heroes."

"Sounds dorky," Spencer mumbled. He hated nerds.

"I know, right? They're all a bunch of North Town brats with rich parents. That's how they got the money to build this place."

"I hate spoiled rich kids. They think they're better than everyone else." Buck's mouth finally started working. He practically growled when he talked. He was tough, slow, and mean.

Smitty stepped down from the platform. "We should let them know we were here. Leave them a little... *present*."

"Let's break some stuff!" Spencer said as he flipped a bench over. Then he kicked a table several times, trying to bust it apart.

"Maybe I should poop on this platform. That would be a nice gift." Buck started unbuckling his belt.

"Let's hold off on the poop, Bucko." Smitty lit one of the wall torches. "I've got a better idea."

Spencer walked over to the stack of boxes and crates piled up in front of the south wall. He pulled one of the crates down and smashed it on the floor, journals and pens spilling out.

"What a bunch of geeks. What kind of a club gets together to write in their girly diaries? I bet they play with dolls, too. I bet that when they meet, they like to..." Spencer froze for a few seconds trying to make sense of the glowing white disc of light embedded in the wall behind the boxes. The portal softly hummed and glowed as Spencer just stared.

"What the heck is that!" Buck was stunned. He'd never seen something so magical.

"That is the door to the Chamber of Crossroads. And that is where our journey will take us next," Smitty said calmly.

"Uh-uh. We ain't goin' in there. We're staying here," Spencer said.

"What's a matter, Spence? You chicken? Are you *scared*?" Smitty knew how to push their buttons.

"I ain't scared of nothin'. But we ain't stupid, neither."

"Sure you're not." Smitty walked over and grabbed the torch ensconced on the wall. Both bullies watched him as he strode over to the big, yellow curtain and held the torch to the hem at the bottom. In an instant, the curtain was blazing. The fire lit the room with a sick, wavy, orange light. The heat slowly intensified. Smitty still held the torch and walked over to the portal. He turned around and said, "When you're done peeing your pants, I'll be in here." Smitty dropped the torch on the floor by the boxes and crates. The flames crawled up the stack. Both bullies watched in horror as Smitty stepped through the portal and disappeared, leaving them in a burning clubhouse.

The heat and panic did the trick. The twins ran for the portal and dove through head first. They bumped their heads together as they tried to cram themselves through the white disc at the same time. They were so big they almost didn't fit. The portal was big enough for one boy to easily pass through at a time, but it was a tight squeeze for two chubby teens.

The stones on the floor of the chamber were cold. It was a welcome relief to the heat of the blazing clubhouse. As they picked themselves up, they could smell the smoke coming through the portal, though they couldn't see or hear the inferno.

"Welcome to the Chamber of Crossroads." Smitty stood with his hands on his hips and his back to them, taking in the sight of the giant domed room.

Spencer and Buck stood still with their mouths hanging open again. More dumb stares from their wide hazel eyes covered their faces. The center of the chamber commanded their attention. A giant scraggly tree with bare branches stretched its limbs upward and held aloft a giant, glowing, green crystal. The light from the glowing stone filled the chamber and made their skin look pale, like zombies.

"Well, that's new. Weird." Smitty approached the tree and slid his palm over the trunk. When he saw the wooden face, he recognized it immediately.

"Dewin!" he gasped.

"Do what?" Spencer found his voice finally.

"I said *Dewin*. He was a friend of mine once." Smitty was a little sad to see the old green wizard reduced to this lowly state.

A low thunder rolled through the room. A humid icy wind blew as strange noises that sounded like moans and screams came from above. All three boys looked up and saw the black portal in the ceiling. Dark smoke swirled and churned as four long, smoky tentacles slithered out and reached downward.

Spencer peed his pants and fell to his knees in fright. Buck was motionless and terrified, but he didn't need to go to the bathroom... anymore. He was running on empty. Smitty was scared, too. But he knew that his new friends, his *true* friends were ready to serve him. They needed his help and told him exactly what he must do.

He turned his back to the tree. The crystal behind him cast not one, but two shadows out on the stone floor.

"MALEK!" Smitty shouted to the portal above. A flash of lightning and a crash of thunder replied. "I give you my shadow. You are RELEASED!"

One of his shadows took on a life of its own and leapt from his feet. It crawled forward directly under the black portal. A bolt of lightning struck the shadow and a spray of sparks flew in every direction. The shadow stood upright with a three-dimensional form of a man. He stood facing Smitty and waited.

Smitty's heart pounded, but he continued.

"TROLLKARL!" Smitty shouted, a little less boldly this time. "I give you my shadow. You are RELEASED!"

The other shadow followed suit and crawled away from him. The lightning did its work, and the other shadow stood right.

Side by side, they stood motionless. The thunder and lightning stopped, and the wind ceased to blow. The chamber was silent, and the light had changed. The glowing green crystal had changed its color and filled the room with a deep red light. Smitty looked up over his shoulder and beheld the giant crystal being clutched by the Dewin tree. It had the appearance of an enormous red ruby.

"Did you bring them to us?" Malek's voice boomed through the chamber.

"Yes. They're over there." Smitty pointed towards Spencer and Buck.

"Me first." Trollkarl's voice sounded like steel swords scraping against one another. "I want the big one." Trollkarl's shadowy arm stretched through the air and wrapped around Buck's torso. Buck's own shadow leapt from his feet and was swallowed into Trollkarl, making his human form just a little bit larger. Buck dropped to the ground and moaned.

"What's happening?" cried Spencer as he watched. "Leave my brother alone!"

"I'll take that one, I guess. The chatty one." Malek stretched his shadow arm towards Spencer. The boy wriggled and cried as well. Both boys were on their hands and knees on the stone floor. Their bodies twisted and bulged and re-formed. Hair grew all over them and their heads elongated. Sharp teeth poked out from under their lips and their moans turned to howls and grumbles. Spencer's clothes no longer fit as his body was that of a large grey wolf. He tore at the tight fabric with his teeth until they were removed. Buck's clothes ripped off by themselves as his body swelled in size. The shredded clothes laid at his enormous, clawed paws. He had become a bear.

"Heel!" ordered both shadow wizards at once. Spencer silently padded his way over to Malek and obediently sat on his haunches. Buck slowly plodded his massive grizzly form to Trollkarl and stood on his hind legs briefly, before clumsily sitting beside the wizard.

"Now..." Smitty interrupted. "It's time for you to keep your end of the bargain. You are bound to me. You promised riches and power, remember?"

Malek and Trollkarl nodded their dark heads in unison.

"Who do you serve?" Smitty said in a commanding voice.

"Petros o Magos," the wizards replied in unison.

Smitty smiled. "That's right. Me." With a quick hop, Smitty climbed into the Dewin tree and scaled its branches to the top. He pulled a small pocket knife from his pocket and chipped at the glowing red crystal. Within a few seconds, he had broken off a foot-long shard. He hopped down from the tree and faced his servants.

"Follow me."

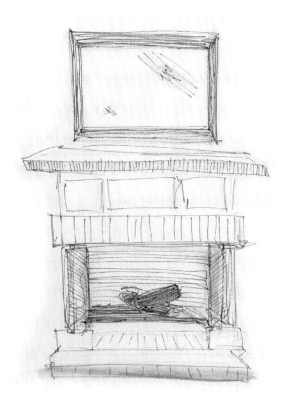

Regrouping

Toby sat in his bedroom, staring out the window above his desk. A heavy fog had lifted just enough for him to see the hazy outlines of his neighbors' houses. There was no wind to drive the fog away this morning and everything seemed still as it laid hidden in the gloomy fall morning.

When a car rolled by, the fog would swirl and dance around it, slowing its motion and twisting into odd patterns. Several times, Toby thought he saw one of his old friends, one of the Travelers walking down the sidewalk through the fog. But they were just flickers of his imagination, bringing back memories and feeding his anxiety. He had been worrying about Traveler's Rest and the five worlds. Smitty had taken the timepiece and had free and unchecked access to the Chamber of Crossroads. Toby felt sick inside knowing that every single member of the Traveler's League was now back at home in the six thirty. No one was left to guard the chamber or the clubhouse. *I'm so stupid. What a careless thing to do.*

Toby had been held in the city jail for several days while he waited to hear what the court would do to him. He had been charged with attempted kidnapping. Smitty had outfoxed him. Checkmate. But when Smitty disappeared again, along with two other Old Town boys a few days later, the police realized that Toby, who sat in a jail cell, couldn't be involved. Toby was released and told to stay at home under the supervision of his parents. Even though he was innocent, the judge didn't care much for teenagers and forced Toby to complete the school year at home. This made it hard to talk to Eli, Aiden, Thomas, Christian, and all the other Travelers that went to the same school. Most of his evenings were spent texting his friends or chatting online.

Eva Mae had disappeared too, but the news channel didn't talk about it, and nobody at school had any idea. Nobody cared about some unknown orphan girl disappearing. *I hope she's okay. Good thing GeriPog is with her.*

"Toby!" his mom's voice called from downstairs. "It's time to go."

"Yeah. Okay, Mom." Toby grabbed his brown leather jacket and slipped it over one arm as he bounded down the stairs.

"Are you sure this is okay? I mean the judge didn't seem like she liked me all that much."

Toby's mom reassured him, "It's fine. You're not allowed to get close to the school. She didn't say anything about the park. And she didn't say you couldn't spend time with your friends. You just have to be supervised. At all times."

Toby's mom thought the judge had been too harsh on her son. It was obvious he was innocent and had done nothing wrong. He had been playing with that red-headed troublemaker from Old Town, and the little punk had his feelings hurt and decided to get back at her son.

"If I ever get my hands on that kid..." Toby's mom said a dozen times a day. "I'm going to wring his little neck."

"Yeah. Sure, Mom. I'll be sure to visit you at the prison every Saturday, too," Toby snickered. "I hope you like stripes. It's all you'll be wearing for the next, like, fifty years."

They laughed together as they plopped into her car and buckled up.
The drive to the park was quiet. The morning fog had almost completely lifted and only the very tops of the trees were still hidden. When they parked the car, they walked side by side to the center of the park and sat on one of the benches facing the beautiful, gurgling fountain.

"So this is where I got arrested," Toby said, almost bragging.

"Tell me again exactly what happened," Toby's mom pleaded.

He had been careful not to tell his mom too much about the timepiece, and definitely not about the worlds beyond their own. She wouldn't believe it.

"Come on, Mom. I've told you a thousand times. We were goofing off between classes and I found this pocket watch laying on the ground. Smitty wanted it and we argued over it. Things got heated, *because he's such a jerk*, and he pushed me. I lost my cool and smacked him, and he got his feelings hurt. He spread lies about me and when the teachers got wind of it, they called the cops. I was being held in the principal's office but ran off when I heard them say they were calling the police. And this is the spot where Officer Sanchez cuffed me."

"But what about all the fliers all over town? I heard they had been looking for you for a while." Toby's mom didn't believe a word of his story. She knew there was a deeper explanation but couldn't get him to share it.

"The Old Town boys helped Smitty make a bunch of copies and put em up all over town. They probably played hooky all day."

She didn't press any more. It was obvious Toby agonized over his ordeal. She hated the thought of her son feeling like an outcast. That's why they were at the park, so Toby could say hi to his friends.

A few minutes later, a familiar face came down the path that led to the playground.

"Hey, Cap!"

"Eli! What's up? Did you tell Christian and the others?"

"I did. They should be here…"

"Hey, Cap!" Christian rounded a corner and came into view with Aiden, Thomas, and Hoops.

"Good to see you guys." Toby felt like himself again, the captain of the Traveler's League. "Mom? We're going for a walk. Is that okay?"

"Fine. Just stay in the park." Toby's mom pulled a book from her purse and settled in for some alone time.

Toby and the boys hurried off, talking as quietly as a gang of boys could. When Toby felt like he was far enough away from his mom or anyone else in the park to hear, he stopped. Facing the group, he said, "We got a real problem. Smitty hasn't returned in weeks. I'm worried about what he might be doing."

The boys all nodded but only Christian spoke, "Well, GeriPog and Eva Mae are still there. So, at least Sirihbaz is still safe... hopefully."

"Hopefully. But I have a bad feeling that Spencer and Buck are with him."

"The Old Town boys?" Christian *hated* those bullies. He'd lost many lunches to them and had even received a few bruises in the past.

"I'm sure of it," Toby continued.

"And now that Traveler's Rest is unguarded, I'm sure Smitty and the twins went straight to the chamber. They can go in and out of any world they want. By now, he probably knows the location of every portal." Toby thought for a few seconds, trying to get some kind of plan together.

"They may even know where the portal to the six thirty is hidden," Eli suggested.

"I don't see why they'd come back here," Aiden piped up. "Everyone here can't stand them."

"Revenge." Thomas rarely spoke. But when he did, he practically growled. He was a quiet and angry twelve-year-old who had been bullied for years because he was kind of fat. But now that he was hitting puberty early, and had a couple of hairs on his chin, other kids messed with him a little less. And he was the toughest kid in the group, hands down.

"Thomas is right," Toby replied. "We need to be on the lookout. If Smitty shows up here, we have to do everything we can to get the timepiece back... even if it means we break the law. I won't hold it against you if you're not up to it."

"We're all with you, Cap," Christian reassured him. "If I see the fox, or his two goons, I'll punch him so hard, his..."

Christian looked over Toby's shoulder and his eyes got wider and wider. He couldn't talk and had a confused look on his face.

"What's wrong, Christian?" Toby asked.

The leader of the Club Knights slowly raised his arm, pointed over Toby's shoulder, and said, "How in the heck…"

Toby spun around to see what was so startling. Down the path next to the playground, Eva Mae walked towards them. Next to her was GeriPog, in *normal* clothes. But people still stared.

When she got close, it was obvious something was wrong.

"Eva Mae! How did you get here?" Toby was stunned.

Her eyes were red, and her nose was runny. She had been crying. She ran to Hoops and threw her arms around him.

GeriPog caught up a few seconds later. He looked at Toby and said, "Sirihbaz has fallen."

Planning in the Park

"What the heck happened? How did you get here?" Toby reeled with confusion. "Where's Smitty? What do you mean *Sirihbaz has fallen?*"

"I couldn't stop them. I wasn't powerful enough." Eva Mae looked tired and her eyes were red.

GeriPog glared at Toby. "That fox kid I trapped, he got into Sirihbaz. Everything is destroyed. Burned to the ground. Half the forest is still a blazing furnace. The castle is still there, but only the stones, and that dragon scale roof, of course. And the sky... it's gone dark. There's no light. It's like the sun was never there. It's just *gone.*" GeriPog poked his fat forefinger in Toby's chest. "You were supposed to get rid of him. Bring him back here. I thought you could handle the little task of ridding us of that vermin."

Toby was stunned from the news and felt the shame of his failure. It wasn't his fault that Smitty escaped from him and stole the timepiece, but Toby knew that true leaders accept responsibility for failures that happen when they are in charge.

"What do you mean 'the sky is gone?'" Eli asked.

"Not the sky, Keeper. Scrape the wax out of your ears. The *sun* is gone. There's no light in the sky anymore." GeriPog turned and squarely faced Toby. "Half of my people are dead!" He was practically shouting as he continued to poke and push Toby backwards down the path. "The other half are hiding in the Crystal Mines. Probably starving to death, and it's *your fault!*"

"Stop it, GeriPog! It wasn't Toby's fault. Smitty lied to the police and had him arrested." Christian wouldn't tolerate his captain being pushed around and openly accused.

"NO. He's right," Toby said calmly. "It's my fault that Smitty escaped. I was careless when I came back. And it's my responsibility to fix things… somehow."

GeriPog wasn't appeased much. "He's not alone. It's worse than you think."

"I know. He's got two other boys with him. I know them. They're bullies."

"Don't put words in my mouth, boy! You need to listen. Maybe learn something. I didn't see any boys with him." GeriPog stepped so close to Toby that his harsh eyes were looking straight up at the teen's face. "He's released the shadow wizards!" GeriPog snapped.

The boys gasped, and Eli almost fainted. He knew more about the shadow wizards than anyone, except Old Dewin. Eli spent all of his free time at Traveler's Rest reading the journal entries he'd made of all the travelers' experiences. Dewin had often mentioned the shadow wizards as well. He had given the Traveler's League a book called, *The Abbreviated History of the Four Gates.*

Eli moaned. "It's over, guys. We can't stop them. They'll rampage through the Four Gates and Five Worlds until everything is destroyed. Nothing and no one is powerful enough to stop them. When it's all over, they'll go back to Skuggi and recreate the worlds the way they want. But not before they come here first... to the six thirty. That's what Dewin told me one time."

"What's Skuggi?" Hoops asked. Eva Mae stood next to him, holding his hand like a scared little sister.

Eli explained, "Dewin's book says that *Skuggi* is the ancient name for the shadow world."

"The three o'clock world, Hoops," Christian offered.

"The shadow wizards want to restore Skuggi and bring it out of the shadow. But they have to darken all the other worlds first. They need to steal their light and seal their portals." Eli was a walking encyclopedia. "That's what Dewin's book said."

"So, is Smitty being controlled by these shadow wizards?" Toby asked.

Eva Mae answered, "No. They obey him. He has some weird red crystal wand. And they each have an animal slave. One's a wolf. The other one is a grizzly bear. They both have hazel eyes."

"And they use their magic to change people into animals... on the fox's command, of course." GeriPog spat on the ground when he said *the fox*. "And that's not the worst of it. They have a *dragon*."

The whole group went silent. Shadow wizards and slave animals were one thing. But a dragon under the control of their greatest enemy was indeed the worst news they could think about. Toby didn't want the boys to think he'd lost hope. And normally he'd speak up and say something positive to lift their spirits. *But a dragon! I'm not sure we have a chance. I'm going to get these kids killed. I've been such an idiot.*

"So, let me get this straight," Christian broke the gloomy silence "The shadow wizards have been released, people are being turned into animal slaves, Sirihbaz is burned to the ground, Smitty the redheaded wonder brat has the timepiece, AND there's a dragon?"

GeriPog nodded. "That's right, boy."

"Great. Now I need to change my underwear." Thomas and Aiden laughed with Christian. Toby, Hoops, and Eli didn't think it was funny.

"Well, Travelers, it looks like we have our work cut out for us," Toby said. "We'll need every League member we can get to go back with us and face Smitty and these shadow… things. But we have two problems. One, we don't know where the portal is located in our world, or if it's safe to get all the traveler's through it. And two, we don't know how to stop the shadow wizards, or that dragon. I *know* we can stop Smitty, somehow. But the rest? We'll have to deal with them once we've gotten rid of the fox." Toby also spat when he said *the fox.*

Eva Mae chimed in, "I know where the portal is. We can take you there. It's not too far."

"But an army of fifty kids marching through this town on their own with an old scarred dwarf could raise some eyebrows, no doubt." GeriPog was right. It would be a challenge to get all the travelers away from their parents and rendezvous somewhere in the city unsupervised.

"We can figure it out. I'm not concerned about that as much as those wizards. But I have no idea how to stop them. I don't know magic. And I've never heard a traveler ever mention seeing a dragon, let alone deal with one. Eli, do you have any suggestions?" Toby asked.

Hoops jumped in, "The Oracle!"

Eli said, "That's actually a great idea, Hoops. We need to ask the Oracle of Torpil."

"Then I guess we should start there. I'll go ask the Oracle if the shadow wizards can be stopped, and how." Toby was ready to make things right.

"That's a bad idea, Cap," Christian spoke up. "If you get caught with the orphan girl who everyone thinks was kidnapped a few weeks ago, you'll go to jail again for sure."

At the same moment, Christian and Hoops both said, "I'll go." They looked at each other and laughed.

Christian stepped forward. "I'll go and talk to the Oracle, and Hoops can go with me. He's been there before, and you always said it was smart to have a wingman, just in case something goes wrong."

Toby said, "All right, Christian. You and Hoops, go learn what you can from the Oracle."

"Toby!" His mom came down the path. "It's time to go. Dad's going to be home soon, and you have some homework."

Toby said, "Eva Mae. You and GeriPog will have to find someplace to hide and wait until Christian and Hoops get back. Then we can get the League together and go back. You'll be safer here, I think."

"We'll wait for you guys at the portal. It's in the abandoned train station in Old Town. The basement." Eva Mae grabbed GeriPog's hand and started off to the south end of the park.

"Christian, Hoops, you guys will have to message me online when you get back. We'll meet up and put a plan together then." Toby ran off and met up with his mom.

"Well, buddy, looks like we have a real mission again!" Christian was excited.

"Let's meet at the train station tonight. Eleven o'clock. And bring that cloak of yours. The knife, too."

"You got it." Hoops, Aiden, and Thomas took off towards the park, while Eli and Christian went their own way home.

The Six-Thirty Portal

The scariest part about the abandoned train station wasn't that it was made of stone, had boarded-up windows, or looked like a haunted old museum. It wasn't that Hoops and Christian were meeting there in the middle of the night. The scariest part of the station was the fact that it was in Old Town.

Hoops had no trouble getting there on time. He could move quickly and confidently wearing his cloak. That old green thing gave him the advantage of complete invisibility when he slipped the hood over his head.

Christian had a more difficult time once he crossed the tracks into Old Town. He had to travel west along the railroad tracks, keeping to the shadows. And often times, he would find that a shadow was already taken. A homeless person, or a stray dog, or sometimes a spooked cat hid themselves at night. Mostly they wanted to hide from the jungle of crime that was Old Town at night, and the shadows were the best blankets to hide under until the morning brought relief from the violent attention of roaming thugs that controlled the town.

They met on the tracks behind the station. Hoops slipped off his hood and appeared out of nowhere, startling his friend.

"Ah! Dude, come on!" Christian just about peed his pants.

"Sorry."

"I need to get me one of those cloaks, Hoops. Where did you get it again?"

"A WolliPog gave it to me. He was Dewin's friend... and mine. I think Dewin enchanted it somehow, along with my dagger." Hoops slid his dagger out and let Christian hold it.

Christian admired the razor-sharp blue blade and the white-bone handle. A green crystal was embedded in the bone and gave off a slight glow.

"We need to get to the basement. Eva Mae and GeriPog should be here. How do we get inside? Have you checked the place out, yet?"

Hoops pointed to a window on the first floor that had a board pried away. "That's the only way in that I can find."

One at a time, they climbed through the window and into the musty old station. The stone walls and old tile floor made every footstep and word echo. It was impossible to move quietly. It was too dark to see anything and neither of the boys thought to bring a flashlight. They could be heard but they couldn't see. Not good.

Both boys froze when they heard something shuffle on the floor across the room. It sounded like it was getting closer. There was no telling what or who it could be, and both boys were on edge with fear. Christian still held the knife in his hands, gripping it until his knuckles were white. Hoops slipped the hood of his cloak over his head, making himself invisible to whatever it was approaching them.

"There's no need for that dagger, boy." It was GeriPog's voice.

"It's us!" Eva Mae's voice came from the blackness.

When Hoops heard her voice, he slipped his hood off. "We can't see you guys."

"Don't worry about that." GeriPog grabbed Christian's wrist with one hand, and Hoops' with the other "Just follow me. I'll take us to the basement."

Eva Mae held Hoops' other hand and GeriPog guided them through the dark grand entrance of the old train station to a set of stairs that led down to the lower levels. GeriPog could see in the dark. All WolliPog could. That's why they were perfect for working the crystal mines, and how they could travel so quickly through the forests of Sirihbaz. They never tired and they could see in the dark.

As the stairs came to a landing halfway down, they saw light coming from the lower level of the station. At the bottom of the steps, they saw that some old oil lanterns had been lit and set on the ground between a pair of rusty old train tracks. They were spaced about fifty feet apart and went on for about a hundred yards.

"Are we *underground*?" Christian asked.

"Yep. I think this was the first underground train in Grandville. I don't know where it leads," Eva Mae said. Her voice bounced down a long, dark tunnel ahead of them into the dark.

When they arrived at the last lantern, GeriPog said, "We're here." He walked over to the wall and pulled on a creaky old iron door. Light from the room inside washed the tunnel around them with a low golden light. "Right this way, boys." GeriPog and Eva Mae stepped inside with Hoops and Christian right behind them.

The walls of the room were made of the same stone bricks as the station, but all four walls were uncovered, and there was no sign of a portal.

"Where is it?" Christian asked. "I don't see the portal."

"It's here," GeriPog said as he walked up to the wall opposite the door. As he placed his little hand against the wall, he pushed. His arm disappeared as if he were reaching into a cloud. The wall was just an image, not really there at all. The portal was in plain sight, disguised as a wall of stone bricks.

"You boys be careful," GeriPog grunted. "That fox kid is powerful. Don't spend *any* time in the chamber. Get to Torpil. Get your answers. And get back here as quick as you can."

Eva Mae hugged both Christian and Hoops. "Good Luck."

Journey to Torpil

The Chamber of Crossroads was darker than Christian remembered. The giant domed room glowed with a deep red hue from the crystal held aloft by the Dewin tree. It felt empty and quiet, like the abandoned train station they had just come from. The echoes of the great battle against Braxo seemed a distant, waning memory. The air was still, dusty, and cold. It was so cold, Christian and Hoops could see their breath.

The portal to Torpil, the seven o' clock world, was the next one over from the six thirty portal. Between the two portals were the great double doors that led to the Labyrinth. They had been shut tight ever since Hoops had struck a bargain with Sentinel, the great minotaur that guarded the chamber and the ancient secret green crystal. That crystal was now glowing an evil red and was also not really much of a secret anymore.

Hoops stopped in front of the glowing disc that would take them to Torpil, but Christian passed it altogether and was headed towards the opposite end of the room.

"Where are you going? This is the right one." Hoops' voice echoed off the walls.

Christian turned his head and talked over his shoulder, "Traveler's Rest. I need a weapon. You have that cool knife. And your 'cloak of awesomeness.' I have nothing but two quarters, pocket lint, and pretzel crumbs."

Hoops ran to catch up. And together they jumped through the eleven o'clock portal to their clubhouse.

It was a horrible site. Only the blackened frames of two tables were recognizable. Everything else was a pile of gray ash and charred wood. All of Eli's storage was gone. The books, journals, food—everything was burned up and destroyed. The only light came from a single torch on the west wall above the platform. The boys stepped carefully throughout the room, looking for anything that may be useable.

"Toby is going to flip out," Christian said as he flipped over some blackened boards.

"It's weird. Everything has been burned but the air in here is so cold." Hoops stepped up onto the platform to grab the torch. "Ew! Gross. Dang it!"

Christian walked over to Hoops. "What is it?"

Hoops looked down at the pile of poop he'd just stepped in.

"I don't think that's dog poop, buddy. That's from a person." Christian gagged when the smell of it hit his nostrils.

"Why would Smitty do that?" Hoops whined.

"I don't think it was Smitty. Didn't Toby say something about two boys? I bet it's the Old Town Twins. From the size of that turd you're scraping off your shoe, I'd say it was Buck."

"I hate bullies," Hoops grunted angrily as he continued to wipe the bottom and sides of his shoe along the burnt wooden edge of the platform.

"Yeah. Me too." Christian continued digging. "Ah! Here we go!" He pulled a big burnt plank to the side and slid out a steel longsword from under the rubble. "The handle is a little dirty, but it looks like it's in good enough shape. I'm sure there isn't a scabbard left anywhere." Christian slid the blade through the belt holding up his blue jeans. "Let's go to Torpil, now."

The boys took one last look at Traveler's Rest before they went back into the chamber. When they returned to the seven o'clock portal, Christian turned to Hoops and said, "I have no idea where this goes. I've only traveled to Torpil one time, when I first had the timepiece. I never spoke to the Oracle. As a matter of fact, I don't know exactly where the Oracle is. All I remember were the earthquakes."

Hoops said, "I've been there twice. The Oracle is, well, it doesn't have a lot of patience. And I don't think it likes visitors. You have to ask the right questions, then leave as soon as possible."

"You get me to the Oracle, and I'll ask the questions."

Hoops stepped through the portal to Torpil first, then Christian. It took a few seconds for their eyes to adjust.

They had stepped into a sheet of fog. Though they couldn't see the ground under their feet, they could feel the squish of mud and feel the cool water seeping into their shoes. Unseen crickets all around chirped and sang like an insect orchestra. The fog around them was illuminated by only the stars above.

Hoops and Christian sloshed their way forward until they stepped up on a dry bank. The fog held just over the wet ground, so when they reached the bank, they came out of the blanket of grey cloud that hovered over the bog. They were surrounded by a forest of trees. They had the appearance of maples, with pointed leaves, but were growing the crystal fruits containing the memories of great deeds and brave travelers.

"We should be close to a canyon," Hoops said. "Once we find it, we can follow it to the mountain."

"I remember this place, Hoops." Christian plucked a crystal orb from a nearby tree. As he placed both hands on it, a light within flickered, and an image of a girl with pigtails appeared. "It's Eva Mae!"

"What's she doing?" Hoops stepped alongside Christian as they watched together. "Let me see."

The image was of Eva Mae stretching out her arm with a look of anger and fear on her face. The crystal flashed and showed a tall pale man in a black cloak grabbing at his throat as he was magically lifted into the air.

"That's Braxo!" Hoops hissed.

The man continued to rise until long, smoky, black tentacles wrapped around him and yanked him into a swirling black portal.

"So, that's what happened!" Christian hadn't been in the chamber when the girl had defeated Braxo, but Hoops had.

"Yeah. It was unbelievable. She's really powerful, but her magic only works if she channels it through anger. It's dark crystal magic."

Christian dropped the fruit to the ground when the scene within flickered out and disappeared. "In the park, she said that she wasn't powerful enough to stop Smitty and the shadow wizards."

"The Oracle will know how, though. Surely," Hoops reassured his friend. "Let's go find it."

The boys hurried through the grove of trees until they came to the edge of the familiar canyon. But with trees stretching in both directions along its edge, Hoops didn't know which direction to go.

"How did you find the Oracle last time you were here?" Christian asked.

Hoops eyes lit up. "The canyon told me where to go!" He stepped to the edge, took a deep breath, and yelled.

"I'M BACK."

A moment later, his echo returned from across the canyon. "YOU AGAIN... You Again... you again...."

"I NEED TO FIND THE ORACLE!" Hoops shouted.

"THEN FIND IT... Then Find It... then find it..."

Christian mumbled, "Thanks for nothing. Here, let me try." He stepped up to the edge and yelled, "HOW DO WE FIND THE ORACLE?"

Christian's voice echoed from across the black chasm below, "FOLLOW THE MOON... Follow the Moon... follow the moon."

"The moon?" Hoops looked up but only saw branches, leaves, and crystal fruits above. Through the limbs of the trees, he occasionally saw a couple of stars, but he had no clear view of the sky. "Maybe one of us should climb up and see which direction the moon is in." But Christian was already halfway up the closest tree. He easily swung from branch to branch and crawled in a way that reminded Hoops of a monkey. A moment later, he was too difficult to see. Branches blocked Hoops' view and the dark night sky had hidden Christian high up in the tree.

The leader of the Club Knights could get to the top and poke his head above the canopy of leaves. He scoured the sky and eventually found what he was looking for. When he climbed back down, he looked at Hoops with a worried expression on his face.

"We need to go to the right along the canyon wall. I saw a clearing in that direction. It's at the base of a narrow, cone-shaped mountain. I'm assuming the Oracle's on top?"

Hoops nodded and asked, "What's wrong? You looked like you saw a ghost."

"You'll see once we get to the clearing." Christian hurried ahead.

When they emerged from the grove of crystal fruit trees, they stepped into the clearing. It was a meadow of thick glossy flowers of deep blues, purples, and pinks. The luminous petals sparkled and glowed in the darkness. Hoops recalled them being brighter, but they were still beautiful. He glanced up to examine the sky. Stars filled the sky with a dazzling array of colors as before, but he didn't see a brilliant moon anywhere. The strip of soft light that had waved across a portion of the sky was still there, but it had changed from blue to a dark indigo, almost violet color. It looked just like the Aurora Borealis in Hoops' books, only purplish this time. Hoops gasped when he saw the light wave across a black disc in the sky.

It was the moon.

"It's... black!" Hoops knew something wasn't right. Moons are supposed to be bright, and this one was anything but bright. It was dark, as if it had been eclipsed, then brushed over with black tar. It had once been so bright that it illuminated all of Torpil, Hoops recalled, but now it looked like a sad black hole in the night sky, abandoned by warmth and light.

"I don't think it's a moon, Hoops," Christian corrected him. "That's Sirihbaz!"

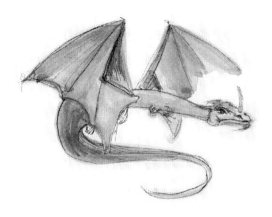

The Oracle

The ground trembled beneath their feet. Pebbles dislodged and scuffled down the path behind them. The boys stopped and held on to the rock wall on their right side. They were halfway up the Oracle's cone-shaped mountain. The path was a stair-stepped trail, cut into the rock along the face of the mountain. It zigzagged back and forth with each leg taking the boys higher and higher above Torpil.

"The cave shouldn't be far. Maybe a couple more turns," Hoops directed his friend, who had been here before, but never found the Mountain of the Oracle.

"That quake was worse than the last one, Hoops." Christian was nervous about getting back down with even more violent quaking.

"I know."

Within a couple of minutes, they were at the mouth of the cave. It cut straight through the mountain towards its flat peak. When the boys entered the opening of the cave, they could see the path curving around the crystal formations and running to the other side towards the opening to the mountain's back side. The dark sky filled the other opening with the glitter of multi-colored stars.

"This place is amazing!" Christian forgot about the quakes momentarily as he wandered through the cave. He examined the stalactites hanging from the cavern of the ceiling. They practically burst with purple gems.

"Hey, Hoops. Those are the purple crystals that the WolliPog mine from the Crystal Mountains in Sirihbaz!"

While Hoops took a few seconds to admire the ceiling of the cavern, Christian set to work comparing them to the stalagmite formations rising from the floor. The dim light from the stars would catch on pieces of crystal barely visible in the stalagmite cones. Christian slid his longsword from his belt and used the steel pommel to chip away at the rock. The minerals easily crumbled away as he worked, revealing the most interesting discovery.

"Hoops! Check this out!" Christian waved his hand, bouncing up and down.

Hoops scrambled over to Christian and looked at the battered stalagmite. Just underneath its surface was a cluster of crystals of various coloring. Mostly, there were purple gems but scattered throughout the cluster were small shards of green, red, and blue crystals.

This was a powerful place, and Hoops knew it. Crystals were the source of magic in the five worlds, and different-colored crystals produced different kinds of magic.

"We should take some back with us. Maybe they'll be useful." Christian pried some of the gems away with the tip of his sword.

"I think that is a super bad idea, Christian," Hoops said.

"We need every advantage we can get against those shadow wizards. And besides, there's no telling if we'll ever get to come back here."

"Yeah, true," Hoops replied, "but without a wizard to guide us, we could hurt ourselves trying to use those things."

Before Christian could answer, the ground started shaking. The quake lasted for a good ten seconds. The boys forgot about their argument and the crystals altogether and agreed to get on with their mission.

They left the cave as soon as the quaking stopped, taking the path as it continued on to the left, just outside the opening across the cavern. The remaining path didn't zigzag across the mountain. Rather, it wound around the top, like a winding staircase in a castle tower. When they reached the top, the two boys stepped on the flat ground. The top of the mountain was shaped like a crater. It was only six feet deep and a hundred feet across in all directions. The ground was bare, like a desert, with a few small stones here and there. In the center of the crater was the wishing well. It had not changed a bit, despite the violent rumblings. Not a single stone in the well seemed to be disturbed.

Christian walked cautiously up to the well with Hoops right behind him. He placed his hand on the well, leaned over the hole, and yelled, "I've come to speak with the Oracle!"

A calm and welcoming voice bounced up the well, "No need to yell, young man! I may be old, but I'm not deaf."

Christian lowered his voice and spoke normally into the well, "We need to stop a boy named Smitty. He has released the shadow wizards, controls them with some weird red crystal, and has a dragon. He's already destroyed Sirihbaz, and Traveler's Rest. We don't know how to stop him."

"I know all that has happened, and all that could happen, and I see what will happen," the Oracle replied.

"So… what will happen?" Christian asked.

"You ask the wrong questions, young man!" the Oracle snapped, and the ground shook for a few seconds. It was a warning. "When boys think they know the answers, they give up trying to find them. If you knew you would lose a fight, would you bother preparing for it? If you knew you would defeat the shadow wizards, would you bother preparing to face them? I cannot tell you what will happen. You will give up preparing."

Christian was angry, but still spoke respectfully, "Okay, Oracle. What must we do to defeat Smitty and the shadow wizards?"

"Petros o Magos," the Oracle moaned. "He brings darkness and destruction. He brings Malek and Trollkarl. He is fire and chaos."

Christian looked at Hoops. "Petros o Magos? Who is the Oracle talking about? Is it talking about Smitty?"

"YES!" the Oracle boomed. "I have seen his past, and I see his future. Eldur og Oreidu. Petros o Magos. He brings fire and chaos."

Hoops stepped forward and asked, "Oracle, how do we defeat the dragon? He has a dragon, you know."

The Oracle whispered, "Worthington. Welcome back, clever one. You have done well in your travels." Hoops said nothing. He waited for the answer. "The dragon's horn. Bring me the dragon's horn."

"How do I stop Petros o Magos?" Christian jumped back in.

"You will not stop him. You've not been chosen."

Christian was too angry to talk. He wanted to bring Smitty down. And it hurt to hear that he wasn't the one to do it.

"How do we stop Malek and Trollkarl?" Hoops calmly asked. But before the Oracle answered, the ground started trembling.

"They're here," the Oracle shrieked.

A terrible roar filled the air. A monstrous screech, like the sound of a thousand giant bats thundered from all around them. The beating of heavy wings pulsed somewhere above.

"My time has come. Torpil will sleep in darkness," the Oracle whined.

Hoops grabbed Christian's arm. "We need to get out of here."

Christian yanked his arm from Hoops' grasp and yelled into the well, "How do we fight the shadow wizards?"

The Oracle said, "Fight them with their own reflections."

"Christian!" Hoops shrieked in terror as he looked up into the sky. "It's there! It's there! We need to leave!"

But Christian didn't give up. "Last question, Oracle. How will the shadow wizards be *defeated*?"

"The horn. Bring me the dragon's horn." The ground trembled so hard that pebbles were bouncing across the bare ground. The quaking didn't stop, and Christian realized that it was indeed time to flee.

He grabbed Hoops by his cloak and the boys ran for the path that led back down the mountain. Before they reentered the cavern, they stopped to behold a terrible sight. The silhouette of an enormous dragon against the purple ribbon of light hovered in the distance. Its giant, bat-like wings were wider than its body was long, tail and all. The wings beat the air like drums as the dragon hovered hundreds of feet above the forest. Its head was back and jaws open. A column of black flame, and a column of red flame wound around each other as they shot straight up into the night sky. A tar-like sheet crawled across the sky in every direction, blotting out the multi-colored stars, the ribbon of purple light, and anything else that might give light to Torpil. The cavern darkened and the gems within grew dim.

"We've got to get back to the portal before that *thing* sees us. Run!" Christian led the way out of the entrance and the boys sprinted down the zigzagging stone steps to the bottom of the mountain. They made a hard left into the forest of crystal fruit trees, only their passage was slow going. The darkness made it almost impossible to move quickly. The ground shook harder than ever, and what could be seen was bouncing in their eyes. Still, they pressed on.

"We're not going to make it, Christian!" Hoops was beside himself with fear. He stopped and began panting heavily, too stunned and scared to move. He was in shock.

Christian turned back and reached in the dark for his friend. When he felt Hoops' arm, he said, "We'll make it, buddy. Just follow me."

The air pulsed in their ears and for a moment, they could see each other in a red glow. The trees behind Hoops exploded in red flame. Hoops shrieked again, "It's here!"

Christian grabbed Hoops' cloak and tossed it over both of their heads. They huddled on the ground under the cloak. The ground trembled and Christian did his best to keep them covered so the beast wouldn't see them.

"Keep quiet, Hoops." Christian peeked out from under the cloak. The beast had landed in a clearing of burnt trees. From behind the flames, Christian could see the long neck of the dragon bend down. Its head was parallel with the ground and looked this way and that for its prey. Christian could see the slotted yellow eyes shining like gold discs. And on the forehead of the beast was a single horn. It was a long, straight, glowing, red crystal.

"Stay under the cloak, Hoops. Let's move slowly. Follow me." The boys stood slowly, keeping the cloak over both of their heads. They continued away from the mountain and the beast step by step, unseen, for several minutes. At last, their feet found the soggy mud of the bog. Christian peered from under the cloak to see the fog cloud that hid the portal.

"There it is, buddy! Let's go!" The boys yanked the cloak off their heads and dove into the thick fog.

The roaring and pulsing of the dragon in the forest behind them was cut off when they slipped through the portal and tumbled onto the cold stone floor of the Chamber of Crossroads. They were sopping wet, exhausted, and trembling with shock. But they were alive!

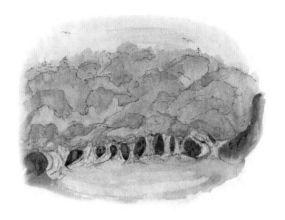

Muster the League

"It's worth the risk." Toby paced back and forth in front of the fountain. Eli watched him with a nervous expression.

"But, Captain, the judge said you had to be supervised at all times. If you run off with the rest of us, you'll be arrested when you come back... *if you come back.*"

There was no way Toby would sit at home waiting and hoping for the best while the Traveler's League faced the shadow wizards, Smitty, and that dragon. He would certainly not be remembered as the captain that sat on the sidelines while his friends stared danger and death in the eye.

"I want every member we've got to meet here at the fountain. Tonight. It's not something we're going to argue about. I've made up my mind. I'm going with you. So forget trying to talk me out of it, Eli." Toby gave an intimidating stare. "Now go, Eli. And remember to tell everyone to bring mirrors. We need all the mirrors we can get, wherever they can find them."

Eli nodded and hurried off to carry out the captain's orders.

"What's the plan, Cap?" Christian asked while Toby continued to pace and think. Christian and Hoops told Toby every detail of what the Oracle had said. They described the dragon and its destructive power.

"They're on a rampage through all the worlds. I have no doubt that Smitty will be bringing his new friends here at some point. But he's going through the five worlds in order, it seems. First, he took down Sirihbaz. And within a few days, he made it to Torpil, and now it's been darkened as well. If he keeps doing things in order, then right now he should be headed to Animas. That gives us a few days to muster our forces. We'll meet him in Hapis!"

"Queen Diambi!" Christian jumped to his feet. "Maybe she can help!"

"Exactly. If we can get the League to Hapis, and convince Diambi to join our fight, then we can face Smitty and his horde *before* they try to come here."

Hoops said, "You mean... we should take the fight to them?"

"That is precisely what I mean, Hoops. If we wait, Diambi and her resistance will be taken by surprise, then Smitty will come here last of all and finish the dark wizard's work. If we want to protect the six thirty, our home, we need to take the fight to Smitty and confront him in Hapis."

"What if you fail in Hapis, boy?" GeriPog spoke up. "You could get a lot of kids hurt, or worse. Do you really want to come home and have to explain why some of your friends didn't?"

It was a good point. Toby felt the burden of leadership now more than ever. "It's our best chance of stopping them, GeriPog. I can't think of any other option that feels safer." Toby stopped pacing and faced the dwarf. "And besides, these are more than just kids. We are the Traveler's League, remember? These kids aren't 'fresh off the playground.' They traveled through every world of the timepiece. They have journeyed, fought, and escaped hundreds of times. They faced Braxo and the WolliPog army. They're not cowards! They're experienced warriors and heroes, every one of them. They deserve some respect for what they've done to help you and your people and your world. Every one of them cried when they heard that Sirihbaz had been darkened. And if they're anything like me, every one of them is terrified of this dragon. *But... they know their mission as members of the Traveler's League is to protect the timepiece and defend the Four Gates and Five Worlds.*"

Toby leaned over and put his face so close to GeriPog's, their noses practically touched. "I don't want to hear you talk about failing, again."

GeriPog grunted and kept his mouth shut. Eva Mae sat next to him on the park bench and listened to the plan intently.

"Who is Queen Diambi?" she asked.

Toby didn't answer. He kept pacing back and forth, thinking to himself, lost in his own plans.

Hoops said, "She's the rightful Queen of Hapis. That's the nine o'clock world of the timepiece."

"What do you mean *rightful* queen?" Eva Mae's face scrunched up. "Either you're the queen or you're not, I thought."

Hoops explained, "When I was in Hapis, some friends of mine told me that the Marsh Trolls had grown numerous enough to fight back against the humans there. They've been at war for several years. The Marsh Troll became strong enough to take over the capital and forced Diambi and her followers into hiding. The humans call themselves *the resistance*."

"The Marsh Trolls will scatter like roaches when Smitty and his dragon show up," Toby interrupted, "and with our forces combined with the resistance, we might stand a chance against Smitty."

"What if the Marsh Trolls and Smitty fight together?" Eva Mae asked. It was a fair question, and a problem that Toby was still trying to work out in his head.

"Then we're going to need some extra help. It would be great if you'd join us, Eva Mae. We could use that magic power of yours. What do you say?"

"Yes!" Eva Mae jumped to her feet.

"Not a chance!" GeriPog leapt from the bench. "She's just a girl. And I'll not let her be killed following you into some foolish battle with a dragon."

"I'm going, GeriPog. You can't stop me."

"Oh? Is that so, my queen? I recall being able to stop you quite easily. If it wasn't for me, you'd still be locked up in Braxo's dungeon, eating wormy bread and pooping in a dirty bucket."

Eva Mae put her hands on her hips. "And if it weren't for *me*, Braxo would still be alive and you'd have more scars on that ugly face of yours!"

Everyone held their breath. Eva Mae and her dwarf stared at each other for half a minute. The silence was broken when GeriPog's face split into an open-mouth grin and laughed hysterically.

"That's true, my little queen. It is quite ugly." After a few more chuckles, he said, "All right. Calm down. Calm down. You can go. But I'm going with you *and you can't leave my side.*"

Later that night, all fifty boys showed up. Every single member of the League met in front of the fountain in the center of Granville Park. Toby explained the plan and took a vote. He wouldn't force a single boy to go on this mission with him. Of course, every boy volunteered to fight. Every boy wanted to be a hero.

They marched south together, an army of fifty small warriors, armed to the teeth with knives, baseball bats, hatchets, hammers, and anything else they could scrounge up at home for a decent weapon. Their backpacks were stuffed with snacks and mirrors.

Even at night, none of the thugs terrorizing Old Town dared mess with the armed mob of boys as they marched towards the abandoned train station. Together, they were an unstoppable force.

The Traveler's League was on the move.

Dewin would've been proud.

A Stranger in Hapis

"Lower the drawbridge, Frump." The voice came from the hood of a red-cloaked figure.

The pair of Marsh Troll guards across the moat snorted and snickered. They didn't reply to the man. They only spat on the ground and glared across the gap between the cobblestone street and the prison gate. The prison was a massive stone cylinder with ramparts and parapets at its top. By far, it was the most imposing structure in Hapis, and it was the capital of the Marsh Trolls. The village that surrounded it was made of drab stone houses with dark-wood trim, thatched roofs, and cold smokeless chimneys.

The cold drizzle of unending rain hissed when it hit the red cloak of the stranger.

"Lower the drawbridge. I won't ask you again."

The guards looked at each other and laughed. Their blobby, onion-sized noses jiggled over their hideously rotten teeth. Their oversized, flabby bodies bounced when they chuckled.

"The last thing you want me to do is let down the bridge, maggot. I'll throttle you real good if I get my hands on you," the guard on the left grumbled in his deepest voice.

The other guard also spoke up. "I'll skewer you like a rat and take you home for my supper. I got three little ones starving for some roast rat!" Both guards chuckled some more.

The cloaked man changed the tone of his voice and in the most polite angelic voice, said, "If you please, kind sirs. May I *please* cross this bridge? You guard it sooo well. It would be most appreciated."

The guards jumped to their feet and grabbed their pikes, lowering the spear tips at the stranger.

"MANNERS!" they cried. "How *dare* you talk to us like that. You're under arrest!" The guard on the left yanked a lever in the stone wall and the drawbridge swooped down. The tip of it slammed against the cobblestone street and guards rushed forward.

The stranger casually slid a long red crystal, the length of a short sword, from under his cloak. Its red light radiated with a heat that could be felt across the moat. The guards stopped momentarily, unsure if they had made a mistake. As it turned out, it was the last mistake they ever made.

The crystal's light gave the stranger two shadows. And with a wave of the red wand, the shadow jumped from his feet and raced forward along the bridge towards the guards. In a flabby panic, the Marsh Trolls retreated, moving their dumpy bodies as quickly as they could to the closed iron doors behind them.

"Let us in! Help! Open the doors! We're under attack! Help!"

The alarm within the fortress had been raised and shouts could be heard within. A moment later, the iron double doors creaked open. The horde of fat, blobby-nosed guards rushed out onto the drawbridge, but all stopped at once when they saw two shadowy figures standing over the carcasses of their fellow guards. The bodies slid off each side of the bridge and hit the moat below with a *splash*.

One guard found enough courage to rush out onto the bridge and thrust his spear at the shadow on the left. It went through the black figure as if he were stabbing air. Malek released an echoing laugh as he wrapped his arms around the guard with ink-like tentacles. Within seconds, the guard had been transformed into a shrieking pink pig! It was a flabby, oversized pig, of course. And it ran for its life past the red-cloaked stranger and down the cobblestone path to the village square. But the squealing was cut short when a huge grey wolf jumped out from between two houses, threw the pig to the ground by its ear, and tore it apart with the fury of a starving animal.

"Now that I have your attention," Smitty calmly said to the rest of the guards. "I'd like to speak with the judge, the warden, and your king."

"Boglack doesn't see visitors," one guard nervously replied.

"Trollkarl." Smitty sighed. "If you'd please..."

The other shadow figure extended his long smoky arm all the way across the bridge and wrapped his black tentacle around the face of the unfortunate guard. With a quick yank, the frumpy troll was flung through the air towards Smitty, landing at his feet.

Smitty removed his red hood and got down on one knee and whispered in the whimpering guard's disgusting, hairy ear, "He does now."

As Smitty strutted across the bridge and into the tower, Trollkarl finished the job of turning the fallen guard into small deer. But the deer had no hind legs and couldn't get to its feet to run. A pair of hazel eyes appeared from the shadow of a nearby house. A grizzly bear emerged and moved towards the deer. Its mouth salivated as if it had been hibernating all winter and now sat for its first meal in months.

The wolf and the bear finished their meals and stood guard at the foot of the drawbridge. No one would enter or leave anytime soon.

Smitty walked into the judge's chamber with Malek and Trollkarl behind him. Behind them, a crowd of terrified blobby-nosed guards followed at a distance.

The judge sat behind his desk, on a stone platform raised a few feet above the floor. When he saw the living shadows walking behind their red-cloaked master, his eyes bulged, and his jaw dropped.

Smitty stepped towards the platform and the terrified judge fell from his seat, landing so hard his white curly wig flopped off his head. Smitty raised his red crystal and touched the wooden desk. It was barely even a touch, more a brush against the wood. The desk was consumed in flames and within seconds, had collapsed into a burning heap.

Just then, the warden burst into the chamber, with a troop of guards behind her. She was two feet taller than the other Frumps and had a long, silver ponytail. She was dressed completely in black and had a face covered in scars. When she saw the judge cowering behind the stranger, and the host of trembling guards behind the judge, she raised a grey-steeled sword with a jagged curved blade.

Pointing the blade at the stranger, she said, "You'll go no further, maggot."

"Ah," Smitty replied. "An escort. How considerate. Take me to Boglack."

"I'll take you to my dungeon, instead. We can play some games. I know lots of fun games." This Marsh Troll was different. She was a real killer. She had attitude, and possibly a quicker wit than most Frumps. Smitty liked her right away.

"Oh, excuse me!" Smitty loved to torment the Frumps with politeness. "I forgot to say *please*. How rude of me.

Where are my *manners*? PLEASE take me to Boglack."

"I should kill you where you stand for using manners on me. Disgusting."

"What's your name, Warden?" Smitty asked with a polite tone. "No, wait. Let me guess... we can make it a game... with that face, and your stunning good looks I'd guess your name is... *Rainbow Sunflower!*"

The warden growled like a chained animal.

Smitty continued, "No? Not Rainbow Sunflower? Hmmmm." He tapped his chin a couple of times. "How about... *Sweetie Pie Cotton Bunny?*"

The warden snarled and screamed at Smitty. But he enjoyed it too much to stop. "Oh, I know! It's *Gut-Munching Beetle-Slurping Wort-Popper!*"

The warden lowered her sword and a smile crept over her nasty scarred face. A few seconds later, Smitty could tell she was blushing.

"Well, you sure do know how to compliment a Marsh Troll!" She laughed like a sea lion with strep throat. "My name is Krimb."

"Krimb, huh? Well, Krimb, you're going to take me to Boglack right now, or I'm going to burn you, your guards, and this whole fortress to ash. AND if you don't drop that sword, I'm going to use it to lift that gorgeous head of yours off your big, strong shoulders and feed it to my dragon."

Krimb stared at the redheaded teenager for a few seconds, then dropped her sword. With a look of surrender, she muttered, "Right this way."

"Thank you, Krimb. You are as helpful as you are beautiful." Smitty and his shadow wizards followed the warden up to the grand chamber of the fortress. The frightened horde of obedient Marsh Trolls followed.

King Boglack

The grand chamber sat at the top of the fortress, the last level of the giant, winding staircase would stop at before arriving on the roof. It was an oversized room that required dozens of torches to remain lit in addition to its monstrous chandelier. These were kept blazing at all times; the Marsh Troll king was afraid of the dark.

Smitty and the shadow wizards followed Krimb to the top of the tower. There they waited as Krimb knocked on the chamber doors. *Bang. Bang. Bang.* Krimb's meaty palm thudded against the wood.

Boglack sat at the head of his long dining table by a stone hearth. Undisturbed by the knocking, he ignored it and continued feasting on his toad and rat casserole.

Bang. Bang. Bang. Again, Krimb knocked. The king grunted, "Bug off! I'm eating."

From behind the wooden door, Krimb's voice called out, "Oh great and gruesome king. It's me, Krimb."

The king's head raised up from his bowl. A frog leg dangled from his mouth as he yelled, "Warden? Is something wrong? Is there an escape? Can't you do your job without interrupting my supper? I said BUG OFF!"

"I have an important visitor, sire. You will want to meet him," Krimb shouted from behind the door.

The king didn't care for visitors. And he hated being interrupted while he was having his supper. He grabbed a mug of vintage cow snot and hurled it across the room in anger. It thudded against the door as he screamed, "NO VISITORS."

Boglack's temper tantrum was met with silence. The king's guards stood on both sides of the door, the one on the left was covered in the snot from the mug. The one on the right picked the mug off the floor and returned it to the table, refilled it, and placed it before the king before returning to his post.

Suddenly, the glow and warmth from the hearth went out. The flaming logs crumbled to ash, and the fire that had been blazing only moments before flickered out, as if someone had flicked a light switch.

"Guard!" Boglack shouted. "My fire." The guard hurried over to the hearth and tried to start a new fire but was unable to get a flame going at all.

"What's your problem, you toad? Can't you even start a small fire? You can't do anything right," the Frump king scolded.

"It's too cold, sire. Nothing will catch. The stones and logs are cold as ice." The guard's breath was visible as he whined to the king, and he shivered. His fat, swollen hands trembled from the cold as he kept trying to please the king with new fire. "It's s... s... some kind of w... w... witch... c... c... craft."

"Nonsense. Ain't been no witches in Hapis for centuries. The humans burned them all. Don't you read your history books?" Boglack snapped. The grumpy king was fed up with the fire, and food. He stood his flabby body up and in a fit of spoiled blobby brattiness, flipped the long dining table over. He waddled over to his throne and plopped down with a grumpy sigh.

As the guard was busy cleaning up after the king's tantrum, Boglack stared at the chamber door. A long, black shadow slid under the door into the room. It slowly crawled across the floor and stopped halfway between the chamber doors and the throne. The king's eyes were wide with fright. He watched in frozen terror as another shadow slipped under the door and moved across the room, stopping next to the first. Then, both shadows stood straight up and materialized into identical three-dimensional forms of two men.

The king trembled as the shadow wizards stood before him motionless.

"I think you should open the door, Boglack," a voice called from behind the wooden chamber doors, but it wasn't Krimb's. It was the voice of a young human.

The king was too scared to talk, or run, or do almost anything. His only reply was to release his nervous, irritated bowels. A nasty fart trumpeted from his frumpy butt and the guards within the chamber held their noses in disgust. One guard had seen enough and opened the wooden door for the visitors. A red-cloaked boy with reddish hair strode into the room. He walked with a confident air and stopped between the two shadows that stood before the throne.

Smitty crinkled his nose and said, "Dang, Boglack! What have you been eating?" He waved his hand in front of his nose.

"Who... who... are you?" the Frump king shuddered.

"I'm the new king."

"Guards! Seize him! Help!" Boglack shouted. But nobody rushed forward to help the Marsh Troll king. The room filled up with Frump guards, but they shuffled into the room cautiously, keeping a safe distance from Smitty and the shadow wizards. The Frumps were in no hurry to carry out the king's orders. They only watched and waited to see what this stranger may try to do.

"Guards! Attack! Seize him!" the king shrieked. "Obey your king!" But the guards were too scared.

"You're sitting in my chair, Boglack." Smitty pulled his crystal wand from his cloak and pointed it at the king's blobby, onion-shaped nose.

"Who are you, you devil?" Boglack repeated.

Smitty lowered his arm. "You're right. How rude of me not to introduce myself. I am Petros o Magos." The shadow wizards melted into the floor as Smitty spoke. They crawled up the walls and snuffed out the torches one by one. "I am the Red Wizard of Sirihbaz." More torches lost their light. "I am the Dark Lord of Torpil." All of the torches ensconced on the walls of the chamber had been extinguished. Only the chandelier above gave the room light. "I am the *KING*... of Hapis." A sharp, icy wing snuffed out the chandelier and the room went black. Only the red crystal wand in Smitty's hand gave any light. He held it up between him and the trembling Frump king. Their two faces were the only visible objects in the room. "I am fire and chaos... and you're sitting in my chair."

All at once, the wand went dark and the complete darkness of the room vibrated with the king's fear. He cried and shouted. He shrieked and moaned and begged for light. The shouts and moans turned into sobs as Boglack slid out of the chair and onto the floor.

"Malek..." Smitty sighed. "If you please." The room exploded in light. The torches on the wall, the chandelier, and the fireplace in the wall burst to life with sudden flame. Boglack lay on the stone floor, curled up on his side, crying like a baby.

Smitty stepped around the blubbering Marsh Troll and stood in front of the throne. He turned around and addressed the horde of guards that had assembled, "I am Petros o Magos. Your new king." No one argued. No one protested.

"Krimb, please take Boglack to his new… cell."

"Yes, Lord." Krimb and a couple of nameless Frump guards grabbed the ugly pile of troll flesh that used to be their king, and roughly dragged him kicking and screaming out of the chamber.

Petros o Magos, the fox king had come to power.

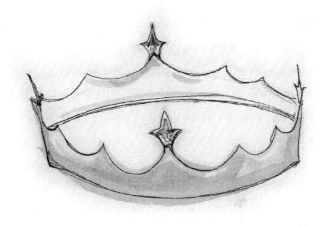

The Resistance

"You're probably wondering why I've come to Hapis." The fox king sat on the edge of Boglack's throne, his hands gripping the tips of the armrests. "I've come to save you from this miserable place, actually. I've come to take you away from the conflict with the humans. I've come to cleanse your world of the rain, and swamps, and filthy forests. And most of all, I've come to usher into my kingdom."

The Marsh Trolls filled the chamber. They lined the walls and filled the room with their big, flabby bodies and bad breath. When they heard Smitty mention a new kingdom, they whispered and muttered to each other.

"But we like it here," said a Marsh Troll somewhere near the chamber doors.

Another cried, "We have all we need. And we've dealt with the humans. They hide in the forests and caves."

"They hide in the swamps and marshes. We've taken the tower, the city, and all of Hapis is ours," Krimb informed her new king.

Smitty stood and raised his voice, "Hapia is a puny world. You have no resources. And your numbers grow by the day. It won't be long until you've eaten everything and begin to starve... or are forced to eat each other." The room was silent. They knew he was right. It was only a matter of time. "I've found a new world. I'm building my kingdom there. It's vast. There's room for everyone. And the best part is that *no humans* will be allowed to live there." More excited whispers filled the room. "Creatures from Sirihbaz, Torpil, Animas, and Hapis will all find refuge in my kingdom. It will be an oasis, free of human scum, and open to all who will help me build."

Krimb said, "It sounds wonderful. When can we go?"

"It's lost in darkness. I need to bring light into my new world, first. I've gotten halfway to my goal, and only need to reap the light of Hapis... and Earth."

"What is Earth?" Krimb asked.

"It's the world of the humans. My home world, actually. Filthy place." Smitty spat on the ground.

The Frump judge stood at the front of the crowd before the throne. His white, curly wig was crooked, and he stood with his neck bent, looking at the floor in humility.

"What is this new world of yours called, the one encased in darkness?" he asked.

"Skuggi," Smitty replied. "I need strong Marsh Trolls to help me build it, and keep the humans out, especially the travelers."

Bang. Bang. Bang. From behind the closed chamber doors, the growling anxious voice of a guard yelled, "I need to see the king! Open the doors!"

"Let him in," the fox king ordered.

An armed guard pushed himself to the front of the crowd and stood before the throne. His eyes were full of fear and his breath was heavy from moving his fat, blobby body down the flight of steps from the top of the tower.

"You need to come see, sire. We have visitors. Humans!"

The entire room grunted and moaned as Smitty followed the guard out the doors and up the winding staircase. The steps took them to the top of the tower. It was a completely flat roof with parapet walls all around. A unit of five Marsh Troll guards were clustered at one end, looking out over the wall.

"Look, sire!" one guard excitedly yelled. He pointed his fat sausage finger towards an enormous field between the town and the dark forest beyond.

Smitty hurried to the edge of the roof and looked between the ramparts. A mass of armed humans stretched out in a line. Then another line of soldiers emerged from the forest behind the first. Then, a third line came forth. From end to end, the lines of soldiers were a hundred yards across. At the center of the front row, a soldier held a long pole with a broad green flag. When the wind caught it, Smitty could see the image of a golden stone tower. Next to that flag, another pole rose into the air. A bright, yellow flag with the letters "T" and "L" emblazoned in red waved in the breeze.

"I can't believe it!" Smitty yelled to the guards. "They're here. The Traveler's

League has come to Hapis." He laughed uncontrollably. "They think they can stop me! Ha ha ha." After he caught his breath from laughing, he said, "I'm going to enjoy this."

Smitty turned to the guard who had led him up the stairs. "Tell Krimb I want every Frump that can swing a sword to form up outside the tower. We're going to have ourselves a little fight today!"

"But, sire, they have Resistance forces with them. Queen Diambi!" one guard warned.

"I wouldn't care if they had the Army, the Air Force, and the Navy. They can't beat me. I have Malek and Trollkarl. I'm invincible. Don't worry, Frumps. The day is ours! We have fire and chaos on our side." Smitty couldn't wait for the moment he would spread his wings and rake his former friends with fire. *They'll scatter like roaches,* he thought.

*****

Queen Diambi stood under the green flag of her noble house. She had waited a long time for the opportunity to face the Frump army in the field, and take back her city, and her tower. But today wasn't the day. That's not why she and her warriors were here. Only the first of the three lines were trained soldiers. The other two lines were the rest of her people—women, children, and the elderly. They were dressed head to toe in leather armor, stained green and dark brown.

"Are you sure this is a good idea, Toby?" she asked. "I'm taking an enormous risk exposing my people to this kind of visibility and danger." Her deep, blue eyes were sharp and cold, contrasted against the warm dark tones of her skin. Her jet-black hair was pulled back and braided, which coiled around her forehead and fastened on the back of her head. A single green gem was lodged in the center of an iron band. That iron band was her crown, and she wore it like she was born with it.

"We need to intimidate the Frumps. If they think your forces are bigger than they actually are, they'll want to talk first." Toby stared across the field at the town as he spoke. *I hope this works,* he thought. The Marsh Trolls' army filed into the field. It was hard to tell how many there were, mainly because of their oversized, flabby bodies. "We just need Smitty to come out and talk first. Then we can nab him and that crystal."

"If the Frumps attack, I've ordered that my people retreat *immediately.* My soldiers will remain to help, but I have to protect my people," Diambi warned.

"If we don't get that crystal, it won't matter." Toby looked back towards the forest tree line. Hidden just behind some hedges was a large, wooden contraption. GeriPog had worked with Diambi's warriors and craftsmen to build a device that would help them face the dragon. But that was the worst-case scenario. Hopefully, it wouldn't come to that.

"Is that going to work if we need it?" Toby asked.

"We'll see." Diambi didn't turn around. She kept her eyes locked on the gathering Frump army across the field. "Maybe you should ask your dwarf, Toby."

GeriPog overheard Diambi and grunted. "It'll work like it's supposed to... *if* your soldiers don't run off in a panic when they see that dragon."

Diambi turned and glared at GeriPog. "My warriors are the bravest in the five worlds!" she snapped. "And we're equipped to face whatever comes our way. You may have noticed our shields."

Toby and GeriPog looked at the odd black plates that covered the shields of Diambi's warriors.

"What's so special about those black plates?" Toby asked. "They just look like dirty tree bark."

GeriPog put his nose close to the nearest soldier's shield and sniffed a long, deep breath. "I know that smell! Braxo's tower smelled like that from time to time, usually when the hot sun would beat

- 117 -

down on the roof... wait! No! I can't be! Are those..."

"Dragon scales, dwarf," Diambi said with a tiny smile curling at the side of her mouth.

"Where in the world did you get ahold of dragon scales? And so many of them?" Toby was perplexed.

"That's my business, boy. Not yours."

Toby didn't ask any more questions. And he didn't really care *how* Diambi had found dragon scales. He was glad that they had an advantage, even though it was a small one.

With the flags waving above them, Diambi and Toby watched the Frump army across the field form a long line. It matched their own from end to end. Toby looked at Diambi, and said, "Well, this is it." Toby headed off for the center of the field. Christian grabbed the banner of the Traveler's League and followed just behind.

Halfway to the center, Toby turned to Christian and asked, "You're sure your Club Knights know what to do?"

"I've gone over it with them a hundred times, Cap. It'll work. They got this."

When the two boys arrived halfway between the two armies, they stopped and waited.

"What if Smitty doesn't come out here? What if he just decides to hide in that tower?"

Before Toby could answer, the Frumps in the front line of the Marsh Troll army stepped to each side. Then the row behind them did the same, as did the row behind the second. Four more rows of Frump guards parted until a clear path was made for their king. A red-cloaked figure walked through them and out onto the field. The hood of the cloak was pulled over the head and a red crystal shard, about a foot or so long was gripped in his right hand.

When the fox king arrived at the center of the field, he stopped about five yards away from Toby and Christian. He pulled his hood off his head and stared at his rival.

"You made quite an entrance," Toby mocked.

Smitty raised his right arm and pointed the radiating red crystal straight at Toby's face.

"Surrender."

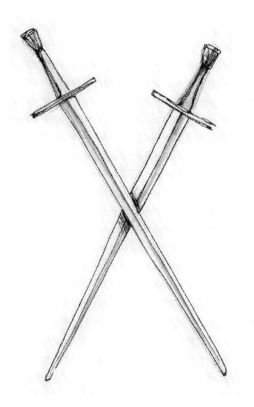

The Battle for Hapis

"Smitty, I've come to apologize to you," Toby began. "You were treated poorly by the League, and I want to settle things peacefully."

The fox king didn't move. He just kept the red wand pointed at Toby.

"Seriously, Smitty. I think that if you...."

"Stop using that name!" the fox king shouted. "Smitty is gone. Dead. I am Petros o Magos."

Toby waited a few seconds then continued, "Okay... *Petros.* I think that if you just explain to the League exactly what happened, they may come around and vote you back in."

"Back in? Ha! I don't want to be in your filthy little club."

"Well, what *do* you want, then? Do you want me to say I'm sorry?" No problem. I'm *sorry!* I messed up. I should've treated you better when I left you in the park."

Smitty barked, "Keep your apologies to yourself. It's over, Toby. I want you and the Traveler's League to surrender. That's the only way you get out of this alive. Surrender now, or I'll unleash my shadow wizards on you and order my army to cut you, the Traveler's League, and Diambi *down!"*

"All right, Smitty. All right."

"It's *Petros!"*

"All right!" Toby relented. "Petros... *King* Petros. I surrender." Toby pulled his sword from his sheath and dropped it on the ground. He turned his head and shouted over his shoulder to Christian, "Drop your sword, Christian. We're surrendering."

Christian acted shocked. "But, Captain! You can't...."

Toby turned around and faced his friend. "I said... *surrender!*" he snapped. He winked before turning back around to face Christian.

Christian did his best to keep a straight face. "Whatever you say, Cap." He pulled his sword out of his belt and dropped it on the ground.

"That's more like it." Smitty sneered at them. "Now, I want the rest of the League to surrender to me. It's time to disband your stupid club."

"Call them over here, Christian," Toby ordered.

Christian turned around and lowered the flag, signaling the Traveler's League to leave the ranks of Diambi's army and walk to the center of the field. Each boy carried a small shield covered in cloth, and a weapon of some kind.

"Tell them to drop their weapons, Toby," Petros ordered. Toby did as instructed and shouted back at the approaching boys to drop their weapons. All fifty boys did as their captain ordered and dropped their weapons in the grass as they walked... but not their shields.

When the boys gathered behind Toby, he turned around to address them, "This is King Petros o Magos. He was once known to us as 'Smitty.' He has taken over the chamber, he holds the timepiece, and is powerful enough to destroy us. We've come to an agreement though, me and Smi.... Petros. He'll let us live and go home, but we have to disband the Traveler's League and surrender."

The boys stared quietly at Toby. Nobody argued or protested.

"We're with you, Cap. Whatever you think is the right thing to do. We're on board," Christian spoke up. The boys of the Traveler's League all tried to look as sad as possible as they formed a long line in front of Smitty.

"To show Petros that we surrender, I want you to all get down on one knee." The boys obeyed Toby and knelt.

Toby turned back around and faced Smitty. "How's that?"

"Not bad. It's a good start, I guess." Smitty lowered the crystal in his hand.

"Good," Toby said. "Now, if you don't mind... *give me that crystal!*" Toby quickly grabbed his sword from the grass and pointed it at Smitty. The fox king looked stunned only for a moment. When he realized Toby was up to something, he raised his crystal and shouted, "Malek! Trollkarl!"

The red wand grew so bright no one could even look at it. The red glare quickly formed two shadows at Smitty's feet and the shadow wizards came to life. As Malek and Trollkarl stood, Toby yelled as loud as he could, "*NOW!*"

Each kneeling boy jumped to his feet and yanked the cloth of the fronts of their shields. Every shield was covered with pieces of mirrored glass. Malek and Trollkarl shrieked and fell to the ground. Their shadowy forms twisted and wiggled in agony. Their screams were deafening. And as long as the mirrors were close to them, they were helpless, screeching shadows.

Smitty slashed his wand through the air, shouting orders at the wizards, but they wouldn't obey. The boys at both ends of the line walked around behind Smitty. The boys next to them did the same. They had practiced the military maneuver a hundred times, and in one fluid movement, they formed a mirrored circle around Smitty and the shadow wizards.

Petros o Magos was furious and scared. His shadow wizards were weak in the glass circle. He raised his crystal above his head and shouted, "Eldur og Oreidu!" But nothing happened. In a moment of panic, he screamed, "Krimb! Attack!"

A long blast from a bull's horn filled the air and the thud, thud, thud of the Marsh Troll army could be heard rumbling in their direction.

Diambi heard the blast and saw the movement of the Marsh Trolls. She raised her arm and signaled her soldiers to advance. Then, just like she promised Toby, she turned around and ordered the rest of her people to flee back into the forest and hide.

Both armies headed for the center of the battlefield. But the Frumps reached the circle first by just a few seconds. Krimb raised her sword and struck down an unarmed boy holding a glass shield. It was Thomas. His back was turned to the Frumps as he tried to keep the shadow wizards in check. But before Krimb could strike again, the ferocious green clad warriors of Diambi's army arrived and smashed into the Frumps. Diambi was with them. She was holding an iron staff with razor-sharp spearheads at each tip. She moved like a ninja, fighting two Marsh Trolls at a time. Two by two, they fell dead at Diambi's feet. Hoops, GeriPog, and Eva Mae were right behind Diambi as she raced into the fighting, and when they were close enough, all three slipped between two glass shields. But Hoops slid his hood over his head first.

The fighting was fierce outside the circle of glass. Inside the circle, Smitty dodged Toby's sword, and wildly swung the burning-hot crystal at his enemy. It was a duel between two rivals. Eva Mae and her dwarf kept as far away as possible from the two boys and the frightful shadow wizards wiggling in pain on the ground. Hoops was nowhere to be seen.

"Iron circle!" Diambi's voice rang clear above the clamor of battle. Her soldiers lined up with their backs turned to the circle of mirrors. They formed an outward-facing ring to protect the Traveler's League from the army of furious, blobby Marsh Trolls trying to save their new king.

Eva Mae knew it was her turn to help. She stretched out her right arm towards Smitty and squeezed a purple crystal in her left hand. She released her anger and felt through the air until she found Smitty's throat. From across the ring, she lifted him three feet into the air with invisible bony hands. The magic that Braxo had awakened in her, the magic she used to destroy him, had come to serve another good purpose. Smitty's feet dangled in the air as he used both hands to pry away the invisible fingers clutching his throat. But he didn't drop the crystal wand.

As Eva Mae held the fox king aloft with her magic, Hoops searched the folds of the red cloak. Then he searched the pockets of Smitty's pants. When he found what he was looking for, he stepped back and removed his hood.

"Got it, Toby!" he said as he held the timepiece out for all to see.

"Good work, Hoops! Now get it out of here!"

With a nod, Hoops slipped his hood back over his head and dashed unseen back to the forest.

Fire and Chaos

"Kill him, Toby!" GeriPog shouted. The fox king dangled in the air and wouldn't let go of the crystal. Toby knew GeriPog was right. It had to be done. With one firm thrust, it would be over, and they could grab the crystal and set things right. But Smitty had once been Toby's friend. He had been the captain of the League and they had shared adventures. He couldn't just kill a boy who used to be his friend. He felt it would be a cruel way to end things, by simply killing a traitor. Toby felt this wasn't how a captain should conduct himself. Smitty was, after all, just a kid.

And there is nothing brave or honorable in the act.

"If you won't do it, then I will!" GeriPog waddled over to Toby and tried to take the sword from his grip, but Toby resisted him.

"No! GeriPog, stop. We can't do this. We'll have to get it from him some other way."

But the dwarf wouldn't hear it. He kept trying to pull the sword from Toby's grasp.

As they struggled over the sword, the shadow wizards continued to twist and groan on the ground. Smitty's face turned blue from the invisible bony hands holding him in the air by his throat. Eva Mae was getting tired. She didn't have much more anger in her to fuel her crystal's magic. And as she watched the boy kick his dangling legs, her anger was overpowered by her guilt and sadness. Toby was right, killing a boy wasn't the right thing to do.

A terrifying roar broke Eva Mae's concentration. The warriors of the iron circle shouted in fear. One soldier screamed as an enormous grizzly bear pinned him to the ground. With one swift bite, the bear ended the soldier's life then stood on his hind legs and roared again. He swiped his massive paws and came down on another soldier. When other warriors tried to pierce the bear from its side, a grey wolf attacked them, jumping into the mass of warriors and thrashing, slashing, and snarling. The bear's great strength was enough to push through the ring of soldiers, creating an opening for the wolf. The wolf dashed into the gap and bit a traveler on the leg. The poor boy dropped his mirror shield, and the boy next to him panicked and ran. The mirror shield had been broken.

The wolf's hair bristled on its neck as it walked to the center of the ring. Its eyes were locked on Eva Mae, bearing its fangs as it prepared to pounce. Eva Mae released her grip on Smitty and tried to refocus on the wolf, but it was too late. As Smitty fell to the ground, the wolf sprang across the circle towards her. Just before it reached her, GeriPog smashed into Eva Mae, knocking her out of the wolf's path. The wolf thrashed at the dwarf and the dwarf thrashed back. When Eva Mae got to her feet, she stretched out her arm towards the beast on top of her friend. But before she could summon her crystal's magic, the wolf yelped and whined. It fell motionless on top of the dwarf who had buried his knife deep in the wolf's chest. When he pushed himself out from under the beast, he gave a few more stabs to make sure it was dead, then grabbed Eva Mae's hand. They both ran for their lives, back to the forest. Behind them, she heard the growl of the grizzly bear and the screams and shouts of warriors in combat with the beast and the Frumps.

Toby was out of ideas. Smitty stood and pointed his crystal at the captain, but before he could summon any magic, Toby quickly swung his sword at Smitty's head. The fox king jumped backward and tripped over the dead wolf. But he was able to get to his feet to avoid another slash from Toby.

Smitty raised his voice and yelled, "Shield Wall!"

The Frumps fell back to Smitty and lined up in the middle of the field. They stood shoulder to blobby shoulder while Smitty pushed his way behind them.

Toby looked at the remaining warriors and the few travelers that hadn't already run back into the woods to safety.

"Traveler's League! *Retreat!*" Toby dashed back towards the tree line of the forest. He only hoped they'd be out of sight before Smitty summoned the shadow wizards. The boys left the field at once and followed their captain.

Diambi ordered her soldiers, "To the trees!" All of her warriors did the same. But the bear still had to be dealt with. Her pride was too great to let the bear live. And she didn't need it following her and her soldiers into the woods. It had ended the life of several of her noble warriors, and her fury against the beast was irresistible. She faced the bear head-on with her iron spear. When she screamed at the grizzly, it reared up on its hind legs. In an instant, she lunged forward, and, as the bear came down, the tip of her spear found its heart and poked out its back. The beast moaned and fell over dead. Diambi stood over her prize, pulled the spear from its guts, and stood before the line of Frumps.

"Who's next?" she shouted. But none of the Frumps dared attack.

Smitty ignored the standoff. With Malek and Trollkarl back at his side, it was time to show them the full extent of his might.

He raised his crystal into the air and in a bold voice, he chanted. "I am Petros o Magos. I am the Red Wizard of Sirihbaz. I am the Dark Lord of Torpil. I am the King of Hapis. And I bring fire and chaos… *Eldur og Oreidu!*"

The shadow wizards turned towards Smitty and extended their arms. Their black tentacles wrapped around him, covering him from head to toe. Their arms slithered around the boy like black pythons. Smitty fell to the ground, cocooned in a shell of opaque shadow. The shape of his body shifted and contorted. He wriggled and writhed on the ground. The shadow wizards moved in more closely and evaporated into dark smoke, and they swirled around him in the air. Faster and faster they spun, kicking up dust and dirt, until they formed a small tornado of black smoke, hiding Smitty from view. The tornado swelled and grew. Rumblings and groans erupted from within and flashes of red lightning flickered from its center. The twister grew taller and taller, rising above the wall of Marsh Trolls. They were terrified of what was happening and forgot they were supposed to form a shield wall to protect their king. They could hear the guttural moans and growls of something mean and huge from within the black tornado. They'd never experienced magic like this before and the redheaded boy who was their king had promised that powerful forces were at his command. Now to be standing before it, and witnessing the mighty power of the red wizard, they lost their nerves and cowered nervously before the dark and terrible whirlwind.

The tornado spun faster and faster, and the top of its funnel rose fifty feet into the air. The air of the battlefield became hot and muggy, and the red lightning crackled through the smoky twister. With a thundering roar, the swirling smoke faded. Smitty and the shadow wizards had melded into one another, and magically mutated into one enormous creature. A dragon, covered in glossy, black scales, stood on its hind legs, craned its neck out, stretched its black, leathery wings, and filled the air with a deep and vicious roar that shook both the air and ground.

The Frumps forgot about the humans in the woods. They forgot about the battle. They forgot about their enemies. They forgot about their king. With the air around them vibrating with the horrible sound of the dragon's roar, they dropped their weapons and ran for their lives in all directions. Many of them went into the woods. They were instantly killed by the soldiers and travelers hiding just behind the tree line. Others went around the dragon and tried to race back to the safety of the village and tower. One Frump was unlucky enough to be quite fatter than his fellow soldiers and ran too slow to avoid the dragon's displeasure. The great, black, beast came down on all fours with a thud that could be felt and heard from the woods. The scaly neck, ten feet long, struck outward at the Frump. The jaws of the beast snapped up the blobby Marsh Troll, squishing his guts out, then swallowing him whole. The lump in the dragon's throat could be seen sliding down its long neck until it vanished somewhere in the beast's belly.

Toby watched from the trees. His stomach was upset from fear, as was everyone else's. He turned to Hoops and said, "I think you need to go now. Take the timepiece back home. If we don't make it, we can't allow Smitty to have it. That *thing* out there must not get into the six thirty." He looked back into the field when the dragon roared again. "We only have one more move, here. If it doesn't work, we'll run for the portal and meet you back home. Now *go*, Hoops! Hurry!"

Hoops set the timepiece for six thirty and ran into the woods. As he ran, he rubbed the lid of the pocket watch. The swirling electric particles of dust spun around him and a moment later, he was gone.

"Diambi!" Toby called out. He looked among the scared faces of the warriors and travelers but didn't see her.

"Over here, Toby," GeriPog called out. He stood next to the wooden contraption he had constructed. Diambi stood next to him, arming the device with what looked like an oversized spear. "We're ready."

Diambi shouted the order to her soldiers, "Dragon Wall!" The human warriors of Hapis emerged from the line of trees and stepped out onto the field. Shoulder to shoulder, they stood, with the edges of their dragon-scale shields touching. The shields were five feet tall and almost three feet wide, and glossy black.

"Forward!" Diambi shouted. And the soldiers all stepped in unison. The line of shields moved out across the field towards the serpent of black death in its center. Behind them, two lines of five soldiers pulled on ropes connected to the device. From the forest, they pulled the contraption from the bushes and out into the clearing. Diambi rode on the device with her hands on a lever. When the machine was plainly visible, Toby recognized the shape of what GeriPog had labored to build.

"It looks like a giant crossbow," he said to the dwarf standing next to him.

GeriPog looked proud of his work and replied, "I call it the *'fox skewer.'* And it will give that black devil the surprise of its life."

When the dragon caught the motion of the line of soldiers moving towards it, it shrieked in delight. It lowered its body and crouched like a cat ready to pounce. Its long neck stretched straight out a few feet above the ground, and its eyes fixed on the tiny humans moving towards it. It waited until they were *just close enough.*

With the dragon's head low to the ground, Eva Mae, who stood behind a tree at the edge of the woods, could see the single red horn on the forehead of the beast. It glowed bright red and was just over a foot long.

"Toby! That looks like the red crystal!"

Toby looked and nodded. "I think you're right. I'm sorry I couldn't stop all this. You were amazing out there, by the way."

When the dragon wall came within about thirty yards of the beast, it arched its neck back. Its jaw shuddered as it burbled and gurgled for a few seconds and looked as if it was taking a giant breath, then struck out like a coiled snake. Its jaws opened wide and two columns of flame, one red and one black, twisted around each other as they projected towards the warriors. The soldiers ducked their heads behind their shields and hid their feet as well. The flames pelted the shield wall for several seconds before it ended. Not a single warrior was burned or injured. The scales on the front of their shields worked perfectly but glowed orange from the heat of the assault. The dragon shrieked in frustration and belched fire at them again.

While the dragon was occupied with roasting its challengers, Diambi's soldiers had time to get the *fox skewer* close enough to do its work. But when she shouted and ordered her soldiers to stop pulling, the dragon heard her voice. The keen eye of the clever devil recognized the new threat and reared up on its hind legs.

Its long, bat-like wings stretched out fifty feet in both directions. As it pulsed again in the air to take flight, Diambi yanked the lever of the device. With a low *twang*, the six-foot-long iron arrow hurled across the field. But the dragon had just risen into the air and turning its body to fly to the back of the field. The iron arrow didn't hit the chest of the beast as intended. It ripped through the leathery skin of the dragon's left wing, tearing a long gash into the skin. It looked like the sail of a ship that had been ripped by a violent storm. The dragon struggled to stay in the air and landed on the ground with a thud.

"Forward!" Diambi ordered and the dragon wall moved in unison once again. Fox skewer was pulled behind, and they moved towards the dragon again. But the dragon leapt into the air and struggled with all of its might to fly away. With a torn wing, it tripped and bumbled through the sky and out of range. But it couldn't stay airborne for long. It clamored its way above the village and landed on the flat roof of the tower. Out of range of the fox skewer, and safe from the wall of soldiers, the dragon set itself to complete the work that Malek and Trollkarl had come here to do. It craned its neck back again, pointed its black head towards the sky and released its columns of black and red flames, twisting around each other as they raced straight up into the sky. Light in the field and the forest dimmed as the sheet of darkness crept across the sky in all directions.

The dragon had won. Hapis fell into darkness, as Toby, Diambi, the Traveler's League, and the warriors all retreated into the forest.

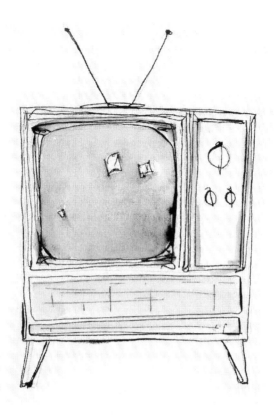

Ghost Town

Three days went by and there was no contact from Toby. Hoops made it back to the six thirty safely and hid the pocket watch. That was his mission, his part to play in the great battle for Hapis. Toby had arranged for him to disappear with the timepiece as soon as they stole it back from Smitty. And because Hoops was successful at this, he felt the battle was going well. But he left before it was over.

A big part of the battle plan was to keep Smitty and the shadow wizards trapped in Hapis. Taking the timepiece from Smitty would make it impossible for him to jump between worlds... unless he found the hidden portal in Hapis. Diambi and Toby knew where it was hidden and worked together to make sure Smitty would never find it. Whether the battle was won or lost, the Traveler's League could, at the very least, keep Smitty locked in the world of the Marsh Trolls for a long time. And time was what they needed. The Traveler's League needed more boys and girls to join. That meant the timepiece must be passed on, and new travelers must complete their journey. And most importantly, Smitty couldn't bring Malek and Trollkarl to the six thirty... or that dragon.

The Traveler's League was supposed to come back right away. But there had been no sign of Toby or his friends, and Hoops began to worry something went wrong. To calm his nerves, he reminded himself that time in our world wasn't the same as time in the worlds of the timepiece. *Maybe they're rebuilding Traveler's Rest before they come back,* he thought. But it didn't help much. The entire city was freaking out. Fifty children went missing in one night, and there was no trace of them. Police questioned everybody. Hoops was even taken to the police station, with his mom, and a chubby detective drilled him with question after question. It was hard not to tell the truth. And after three days, Hoops thought that perhaps the adults could help... but there was no way they'd believe his story.

The entire city was on lockdown, and the mayor set a strict nine p.m. curfew. There were rumors about kidnappings, and Tobias Middleton Sharp was the name on everyone's lips.

"I have to work late tonight, Hoops." His mom was doing her makeup and hollering from her bedroom. "I've asked Ms. Grankel to watch you until I get back."

Hoops didn't mind. She was a nice old lady that Hoops had grown to love. Their friendship had grown ever since he used the timepiece to save her from burglars. That was months ago, and ever since, Hoops would prefer her company over sitting at home alone while his mom was at work.

"Okay, Mom." Hoops went back to his homework and doubled down on his speed. Going to Ms. Grankel's was way more fun if he didn't have to do his homework over there. If he finished now, he could watch TV with her. And Hoops enjoyed shouting out answers to the TV with her. It was their 'thing.'

"I'm leaving in five minutes!" Mom called from her bedroom. Hoops finished the last two math problems and shoved all of his worksheets and textbooks into his backpack. Then he walked over to his dresser and leaned over the cage of his pet mouse.

"Hey, buddy. I have to go over to the old lady's place tonight. Here's some extra treats for you while I'm away." Hoops dropped some special pellets into King Tut's feeding dish. Tut was a mouse. And for a long time, he was Hoops' closest friend. He had even gone on some adventures with Hoops when he began his travels with the timepiece.

Squeak!

"I'm going to lift up your cage now, buddy. Hold on." Hoops carefully lifted the cage off the dresser and looked underneath. The timepiece was still there. It seemed like a good enough place to keep it for now. Next to the pocket watch was his gold medal, with the letters 'TL' stamped on its face.

Hoops set the cage back down carefully and said goodbye to King Tut. He opened his closet and pulled a couple of books off a shelf and peeked behind. The fern and grass-covered cloak laid neatly folded, longways. On top of it was a leather belt and his dagger tucked snuggly in its sheath. The white-bone handle stood out against the dark leather of the belt and the deep green hues of the cloak. In the handle of the dagger, an embedded green crystal caught the light of his bedroom and twinkled. Just one look at that knife and anyone would suspect it was enchanted. Hoops replaced the books and made doubly sure they concealed his most precious treasures. If anyone were to snoop in his closet, they would only find some toys, games, and rows and rows of boring books about science, nature, and geology.

Hoops gave his room one last look, switched the light off, and headed over to Ms. Grankel's apartment. She always left her door unlocked, which Hoops thought was weird given they had to deal with burglars a couple of months ago. One time, he asked why she left her front door unlocked. The little old lady just laughed about it and said, "But my little hero lives next door! How is he going to save me if I lock him out?"

Hoops let himself in and found Ms. Grankel sitting in her favorite chair in front of the TV. Without turning around to look, she said, "There's my little hero! Come over here and sit. Our show is about to start." He plopped down on her couch, kicked off his shoes, and put his feet up.

He stretched out and settled in. When the gameshow started, he forgot about his worries for a little while, knowing there was nothing he could do about Toby and the Traveler's League... other than wait.

"We interrupt this program to bring you a special report..." Channel 13's anchorman blinked onto the television screen. "A national state of emergency has been declared. A strange phenomenon has been impacting the reflective surfaces of mirrors through the country, and the world. It is unclear at this time what is causing it, but the president is advising that all citizens stay inside their homes and refrain from travel. Again, mirrors all over the country are failing to reflect. NASA and the U.S. government's top scientists are investigating the cause. Please do not attempt to travel. Rearview mirrors will not work properly. Traffic accidents in the thousands are being reported all over the country. Conditions are *not* safe. Please stay indoors and do not travel. Also, please do not panic..."

Hoops knew the fox was somehow responsible and worried that Toby and the League may have lost the battle.

He dashed back to his apartment, opened his closet door, and pulled out his grass and fern leaf cloak, his leather belt, boots, and dagger. He lifted his pet mouse's cage. Underneath was the timepiece and his badge, the Traveler's League medal dangling from a red and white-striped ribbon. It was glowing and pulsing. The League was being summoned! When Hoops wrapped his hand around the medal, the room spun around him like a tornado and then vanished with a *whoosh.*

The Best of the Rest

"He's here!" Christian's voice called out as Hoops stepped down from the burnt platform. Traveler's Rest was still a messy heap of burnt tables and boxes, but Toby, Christian, and Eli were hard at work clearing out the rubble.

Toby dropped an armful of burnt boards and walked towards Hoops. "We don't have much time, Hoops. Please tell me you didn't bring the timepiece."

"Nope. I hid it in the six thirty, just like you asked."

"Good. We need to go over a few things before we head back home, and I don't want to take any chances."

Hoops was so relieved to see Toby and the rest of the league safe. "I was worried you guys might not come back. What happened after I left the battle?"

Toby bit his lip and looked ashamed. He hung his head, took a deep breath, and said, "Smitty got away from us. Hapis is darkened… we barely escaped that battle."

"Why haven't you come back home? It's been days since I've heard from you guys," Hoops said.

"We had to help Diambi hide the portal. It took a couple of days because Smitty and the Marsh Trolls were searching the forest for us." Toby's face was half-hidden by the black hair that swooshed over his right eye. "But we should be safe now. I don't think Smitty will ever find the Hapis portal."

Christian brushed his hands together and wiped them on his blue jeans. "Eva Mae and the dwarf stayed behind in Hapis. She said since she couldn't go back to Sirihbaz, she wanted to help Diambi. She said something about *learning to be a queen*."

"Where is everyone else?" Hoops asked.

Toby stared at his own feet in shame and didn't answer Hoops. He only pointed at the glowing white disc in the clubhouse wall that led to the Chamber of Crossroads. Christian had a look on his face of fear, anger, and sorrow, all in one expression.

The hairs on the back of Hoops' neck stood on end as he wondered what terrible thing may have happened. He walked through the portal with Toby, Eli, and Christian following close behind.

He stepped into the chamber and gave his eyes a few seconds to adjust to the little light that remained. The room was awash with a dim, red glow from the poisoned crystal that rested atop the Dewin tree in the center. A stench in the air reminded hoops of the dirty paddocks at the zoo.

"What's that smell?" Hoops asked rather loudly. His breath formed a red vapor as it plunged into the icy air. His question bounced off the stone walls of the domed room and startled the fifty pigs and sheep that had been huddling in a tight herd near the portal. Their bleating and oinking startled Hoops, and he jumped to the side and grabbed his knife, ready for a fight. It was a reflex he had developed since becoming a traveler.

After a moment, Hoops realized there was no danger and slid his knife back into its sheath. "What's with all the farm animals, Toby?"

Toby looked at Hoops from behind his black hair. His one uncovered eye gave away his entire countenance.

"These are the travelers that the shadow wizards caught in the forest."

Hoops was stunned. *It can't be! These are my friends! How could this happen?*

Toby continued, "I couldn't just leave them in Hapis. They'd be troll food for sure. We had to keep sending travelers out into the woods to watch for Smitty and the shadow wizards while Diambi and I hid the portal. When a boy would come back as a sheep, another boy would volunteer to go out and keep watch. That boy would come back as a pig. Then another boy would volunteer to go into the woods. Every one of them volunteered to keep watch and distract Smitty from finding the group."

"They all sacrificed themselves to keep the portal hidden, Hoops," Christian summed it up. "We brought them all back here, into the chamber, and we'll keep them here until we find out how to change them back. We can't let them go back to the six thirty on four legs, bleating, oinking, and pooping all over the place... Watch your step, by the way."

Hoops had already stepped in pig dropping but didn't care. He was concerned about Eva Mae. "I can't believe you let Eva Mae stay behind, Toby! What were you thinking?"

Toby could see that Hoops was angry. He expected as much. "It was her choice, Hoops. Diambi promised to keep her safe. And besides, GeriPog is with her. If anybody can hide and protect her, he can."

"GeriPog said he could keep her hidden. *I can't hide fifty noisy children! I'm only one WolliPog,* he said, like a dozen times," Christian recalled.

"You know how she is, Hoops. She doesn't have a home in the six thirty, and she's really insistent when she gets her mind on something. And GeriPog... he gets all up in your face if you try to give her orders," Eli chimed in.

"For now, we're safe... kids, sheep, pigs, and all," Toby said. "We need to straighten up Traveler's Rest and get a plan together while Smitty is trapped in Hapis."

Hoops had almost forgotten to tell Toby the bad news. "You don't know, do you?"

"Know *what*, Hoops?"

"I thought that was why you summoned me and the League. I thought you already knew and wanted to formulate another battle plan..."

Toby stood frozen like a statue. A bead of sweat appeared on his brow. And his breath puffed out a chain of vapors. "What do you mean *another battle plan?*"

Hoops told Toby about the mirrors. "The two o'clock world has been darkened. It happened just before you summoned me."

Toby's knees gave out. He plopped to the floor and sat cross legged and buried his face in his hands. "It's over. I've failed."

Christian, Hoops, and Eli tried to comfort their captain. But Toby was inconsolable. He crossed his arms, with his elbows on his knees, and hung his head from their sight. They could hear sobs and sniffles.

"You did your best, Cap. Nobody could've done any better," Christian said. He rested a hand on Toby's shoulder and looked at Hoops. "We better get back home. If Smitty's escaped Hapis, it's only a matter of time before..."

"TOBY!" a cocky teenaged voice shouted from across the chamber. "Well, well, well. I'm surprised to find you here, out in the open and all." Smitty had emerged from the two o'clock portal. He slowly stepped towards the boys. As he spoke, he pulled his red crystal wand from under his cloak and raised his arms like an orchestra conductor.

Toby sprang to his feet, tears streaking down his face and anger burning deep within his eyes. He looked at Christian and said, "Get out of here! Get back home!"

"Right, Cap! Let's move, guys," Christian replied. All four boys dashed off to the right towards the six thirty portal. The sheep and pigs panicked and ran in all directions when the boys passed them.

"Malek! Trollkarl!" Smitty shouted as he slowly followed the fleeing boys. The wand in his hand illuminated the room with light. The two shadows the light created at his feet detached and sprang to life. One of the shadows crawled across the floor towards the boys. The other crawled up the dome like a black spider.

"We're not going to make it!" Eli shrieked.

"Just keep running!" Toby shouted from behind them. "I'll distract them!"

Hoops and Eli jumped through the six thirty portal head first, but Christian stopped before he passed through. He turned to look for his captain, but Toby stood at the great double doors that led to the Labyrinth. The shadows moved closer to him. The one on the ceiling was almost to the top of the great iron doors, and the other was only yards away from Toby's feet.

"Toby! What are you doing! Let's go!" Christian screamed in fear.

But Toby didn't answer him. He grabbed the twisted iron handles of the doors and pulled them open with all of his strength. Facing the Labyrinth, he called out.

"SENTINEL!"

The shadows stopped crawling, now only feet away from Toby. The boy turned to face Smitty and yelled again, "Sentinel! I summon you!"

Smitty stopped his walking and lowered his arms. He stood next to the Dewin tree, wondering what Toby was up to.

A great voice bellowed from behind Toby and filled the chamber like thunder.

"TRESSPASSER!"

Smitty knew what was coming. When he was a traveler, he had narrowly escaped from Sentinel with his life. Now the great minotaur would face the power of the Red Wizard of Sirihbaz.

"Trespasser!" the voice boomed again from within the Labyrinth, much closer. And his heavy footsteps could be heard, and he approached.

Toby looked at Smitty with a sly smile, raised two fingers to his brow, and gave a quick mocking salute. As Sentinel came into view down the Labyrinth's great sandstone hallway, Toby dashed to the six thirty portal and dove through with Christian right behind him.

Sentinel charged into the chamber, his black hooves thundered, and snot dripped from his great nose. He had the body of a muscular man completely covered in black hair, and the head of a terrifying bull. Broad leather straps crisscrossed its wide chest and connected to an equally wide belt. His horns were black, sharp, and vicious.

The shadow wizards screamed in fear and crawled back to their master. Smitty waved the red wand and shouted their names, but they were too afraid to detach from him. Sentinel charged closer, and Smitty leapt onto the Dewin Tree and climbed up its bare branches.

Smitty had his hands full.

The Captain Sleeps

The boys fumbled about in the darkness. The lanterns that GeriPog once lit had gone out. It had been days since they first snuck into the basement of the old abandoned train station and passed through the hidden portal. The lanterns were still there, but they had burned through all of their oil. Instead of being helpful illuminating beacons, they were now noisy, invisible, tripping hazards, waiting in the dark to bite at the boys' feet and sound the alarm.

Eventually, Toby felt his way around the room and discovered the metal handle to the creaky, old, iron door that led into the old train tunnel. The tunnel was no less dark, and boys slowly shuffled out of the room with their arms stretched out before them. It was nighttime in Old Town. And even during the day, they couldn't see in the black basement. Their eyes ached from peering into the blackness with no relief of light.

"Hold up, guys." Hoops reached down and pulled the magic knife from its sheath. He felt along its white-bone handle for the green crystal. He held the crystal close to his lips and breathed on it.

The crystal glowed like a stoked ember in a campfire, then dimmed when Hoops' breath stopped. The light from the gem had been enough for them to see stairs up ahead, on the left. Those were the stairs that took them to the main floor, where they climbed through the broken-out window once covered with boards, and out into Old Town's dirty alleys.

Eli said, "That light trick was cool, Hoops! Good thinking. Where did you learn to do that?"

"Dewin taught me," Hoops replied, then turned to the captain. "Remember when he did the same thing when we crossed into Sirihbaz to rescue Eva Mae, Toby?"

Toby was tired. His one visible eye was bloodshot. His eyelid was half closed like he was ready to fall asleep at any moment. His face was expressionless, and half-covered over by his long, straight, black hair. "Yeah. I remember," was all he said.

Hoops continued, "I haven't perfected the spell. But when I do, the crystal should stay lit for as long as I want... like a flashlight."

"You're practically a wizard, Hoops," Eli joked. "Imagine what Dewin could teach you if he was still... well, not a tree."

Christian led the way back to New Town. The boys moved quickly and hurried back to Granville Park. When they reached the fountain in the center, they collapsed onto the park benches to catch their breath.

"So... what's the plan, Cap?" Christian asked, but Toby didn't answer. He had fallen asleep. The sounds of his snores attracted some nearby pigeons for some reason, and they saw fit to land right on Toby's forehead to investigate the sound coming from his nose. They landed on his shirt, and on his shoes, and on the park bench. At least a dozen curious pigeons had come to check out the strange gurgling sounds of Toby's snoring.

Eli clapped his hands and shooed the birds away.

Christian turned to Hoops and said, "You know how we got away from Smitty, right?"

"No. What happened?"

"Toby opened the doors to the Labyrinth and called Sentinel. We jumped through the portal when the minotaur charged into the room! All I heard was him yelling *trespasser* over and over."

Hoops recalled his own adventures in the Labyrinth during his travels and dealing with the powerful beast that guarded the chamber and its secret. "Sentinel is powerful, but he's not all that bright. I'm sure Smitty will figure out a way to trick him."

"Yeah. Most likely," Christian confirmed. "Then he's going to be coming here. It shouldn't be long. Maybe we should wake Toby and get a plan together."

Hoops looked at Toby stretched out on the park bench, deep in sleep. "Nah.. He needs to sleep. You saw how tired he was. He'll be no use to anybody if he doesn't rest up. You and I will have to figure something out on our own."

Hoops, Eli, and Christian brainstormed. They sat on the edge of the fountain, facing Toby, and shared ideas until the sun lightened the early morning sky. The stars flickered out one by one as dawn approached, and as it peeked above the school and washed Granville with its warm, orange glow. The three travelers silently wondered if this would be the last day they'd ever see it rise.

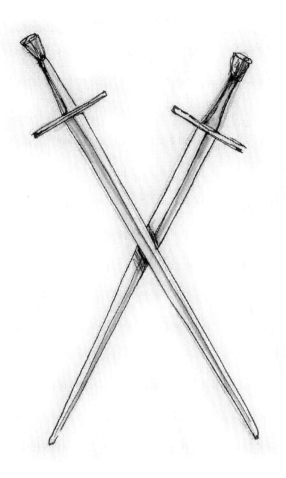

Granville Park

Pop, pop, pop!

Noises came from somewhere south of the park, like fireworks in the distance. It wasn't a holiday, though. And there were no colorful explosions in the sky. Something was wrong.

The boys watched the sunrise in a dreamlike state. But it was a nightmarish dream they couldn't believe: Smitty had won, and now the light from Earth's sky would soon be gone forever.

Pop, pop, pop.

More noises from the south of the park interrupted their sad daydreaming.

Christian asked, "Do you hear that, Hoops?"

"Yeah. It sounds like fireworks," he replied as several more *pops* rang out. "It sounds like it's from Old Town."

All over the city, they heard the whine of police sirens. Something was *really wrong.* A moment later, a police car zoomed by the park. The boys could see it from the fountain as it raced down Walnut Street. Its tires screeched as it swerved around other cars on the street, and its siren blared and moaned. It was headed south.

Eli took it all in and shouted, "Those aren't fireworks we're hearing, guys. They're *gunshots!* The cops are headed to Old Town."

Christian hopped down from his perch on the edge of the fountain and walked over to the bench where Toby slept. He shook his shoulder until Toby awoke.

"You gotta get up, Cap. You've been sleeping for hours."

"Leave me alone." Toby yawned. "I'm still tired."

Christian quickly took one of his socks off and soaked it in the fountain's cold water. He walked back over to Toby, who was already fast asleep again. Christian swung the sock around his head, slinging cold water droplets all around. He walked back over to Toby, then with quick swing of his arm straight down, he slapped the captain of the Traveler's League in the face with the wet sock. Toby sprang up off the bench and onto his feet.

"What the *heck,* Christian! What did you do that for?" he yelled.

Christian grabbed Toby by his shirt, just under his collar. "We need you! Smitty is here!"

Toby came to his senses and heard the sirens and gunfire in the distance. The sounds were getting louder, and they were mixed with other sounds, too. Men shouted. People screamed and ran away from the commotion. A whole crowd of panicked people came around the corner of the school and headed north, away from the danger.

Pop, pop, pop! The gunfire was deafening. It came from an officer who was protecting the crowd from the danger coming around the corner. Even though the boys couldn't see the danger, they knew who it was.

The ground vibrated. The low mechanical hum of heavy equipment came from the north end of the park. The boys turned around to see two tanks on both sides of the park crawling down the street. The squeaky rumbling of their treads, along with the screams of panicked people, made Granville Park feel like a war zone from one of the boy's video games.

"They called in the Army!" Christian shouted. "Surely, those tanks can stop a dragon."

Just then, the danger walked around the corner of the school. But it wasn't a dragon. It was a redheaded teenage boy in a hooded red cloak. Before him walked Malek and Trollkarl. The cop that fired his pistol only a moment ago was busy reloading. Malek stretched his long, smoky arm across the street and covered the officer in black shadow. Within seconds, he was gone, replaced by a mangy dog.

From behind Smitty, a herd of animals rounded the corner and fled from the wizards. Most of them went into the park, some dashed into alleys to hide. There were pigs, sheep, dogs, and the occasional cow. But there were hundreds of pigeons and rats. They all flooded into the park with Smitty, the Alpha of Animas behind them. He too was walking into the park, with his shadow wizard slaves. When he'd point the red crystal wand, Malek and Trollkarl wound pounce on a nearby citizen and turn them into another beast.

Toby nervously looked as Smitty walked up the park's path from the south, and at the two lines of tanks rolling down the streets on both sides of the park from the north. "We better get outta here, guys. NOW!"

The boys dashed off to the north, but not before Smitty caught sight of them.

"Toby!" he screamed. "You're dead! You hear me? I'm going to crush you and your friends! It's over!"

Toby didn't turn back and neither did Hoops, Eli, or Christian. They ran for their lives.

Smitty kept yelling, "I've won! The four gates are closed, and the five worlds belong to me! I am the Red Wizard of Sirihbaz. I am the Dark Lord of Torpil. I am the Alpha of Animas, and King of Hapis. I am the Guardian of the Labyrinth and I bring...."

BOOOM!

The whole park shook, and the air thundered with the roar of the tanks' cannons. The boys fell to the ground and covered their heads. Debris from a tremendous explosion fell all around them.

Christian opened his eyes to see Eli curled up on his side, covered in dirt and Toby crawling over to his friend. "Eli! Are you all right?"

Eli moaned then stumbled to his feet with Toby's help. "What?"

"Are you all right?!" Toby yelled again.

"What? I can't hear you!" Eli's ears were bleeding. His eardrums were busted from the explosion. Toby grabbed his arm and led him north to the end of the park.

Christian looked all around for Hoops and found him pinned to the ground by a large slab of concrete nearby. He rushed over to his friend. "Hoops! Are you all right? Are you hurt?"

He helped Hoops move the chunk of concrete off his legs. He grabbed Hoops' arm and tried to pull him to his feet.

"OUCH!" Hoops yelled out in pain as he dropped to the ground again. "My leg! It hurts. I don't think I can walk yet! I think I sprained my knee."

Christian yelled for Toby to come help, but Toby's ears were bleeding, too. He and Eli kept limping to the north end of the park. He looked back towards the center of the park and saw a huge, smoldering crater where the fountain used to be, and where Smitty had been standing. The air was full of dust and smoke and smelled like gunpowder. One blast from the tanks had turned the town's most beautiful park into a smoky junkyard of torn earth, concrete rubble and snapped tree branches.

Too bad Smitty. I didn't have to end like this, Christian thought as he looked at the dust-filled crater. He knelt and had Hoops wrap his arm across his shoulders. They stood together, and Hoops leaned on his friend as they limped off to find Toby and Eli.

Behind them in the crater, a red light glowed, illuminating the surrounding cloud of dust and smoke. Christian could feel the heat from the red light on his ears and see the reflection of it on the snapped shards of tree trunks. He didn't stop moving, but he did look back over his shoulder as he helped Hoops hop out of the park. Smitty held the red crystal wand in the air, completely unharmed, and covered head to toe in his hooded red cloak.

"It can't be..." Christian gasped. Before Hoops had a chance to look back, Christian pulled him faster and they moved as fast as Hoops' sprained knee would allow. They crossed the street at the north end of the park and ducked into an alley between two apartment buildings. Toby and Eli sat on the ground with their backs leaning against the walls. Their ears rang and couldn't communicate with Christian or Hoops. But Toby saw the look on Christian's face, he knew Smitty was still a threat.

Back in the crater, Smitty saw the dust cloud settle. And before the tanks had another clear shot at him, he yelled out the spell that Malek and Trollkarl had taught him...

"Eldur... Og... Oreidu!"

The Ride of His Life

Red lightning crashed inside the black tornado. Thunder shook the park as loudly as the tanks' guns had only a couple of minutes before. The swirling smoke kicked up every leaf, twig, and branch in the park. The top of the tornado's funnel rose fifty feet into the air. The rush of the hot, dark wind whisked into the alley where the boys cowered as they watched the horrible display of power. They hoped the dragon wouldn't spot them hiding there, behind an old dumpster.

Hoops still wore his fern and grass cloak, and from its hidden pocket, King Tut had crawled out, resting on his shoulder.

Christian said, "That's a brave little mouse, Hoops. Is he okay?"

Hoops grabbed Tut and looked him over. After a few strokes of his fur, Tut returned to his perch, snuggled closely against his master's neck. "He's okay. Just a little rattled."

"I am too," Christian replied, then looked out to the park. "Do you remember the plan we came up with?"

"Yeah. But how's it gonna work? I can't run, and Eli and Toby can't hear anything."

Christian looked at Hoops for a moment, sighed, and said, "It's not going to work. I've got a new plan... I'm gonna need to borrow that knife of yours."

Hoops unbuckled the leather belt that WolliTom had given him. That seemed like a lifetime ago. That was when Braxo was alive and still trapped in Sirihbaz. Christian wished Braxo and his dwarven army were out in the park, and not Smitty's dragon. He'd much rather face his old enemy than the turncoat fox, who had ruined every world of the timepiece and destroyed all but four members of the Traveler's League.

Christian wrapped the belt around his waist and buckled it on as tight as he could. He turned to Hoops and said, "Keep the guys hidden with that cloak of yours. And keep a lookout for me. I'm going after that crystal."

"You're going to get yourself killed, Christian!" Hoops' eyes teared up. "Please don't do this!"

"I can't just sit here, Hoops! Just watch and wait for me. If this works, I'm gonna need you to be ready to travel." Christian opened the pouch hanging from the leather belt. He pulled out the timepiece and tossed it to Hoops. Before Hoops could ask this new plan, Christian had already crossed the street and ran at full speed into the park, towards the tornado.

Twigs and leaves beat against his face as the tornado was now at full force and height. All at once, the swirling black dust and smoke stopped, and the tornado evaporated, revealing Smitty's terrible dragon. It stood on its hind legs but came down with a monstrous thud as it opened its bright, yellow eyes and filled the air with its roar; a sound so thunderous it made Christian's ears ring. He quickly ducked behind a large chunk of broken concrete, possibly from the fountain, or maybe it used to be the sidewalk. He wasn't sure. But it was big enough to keep him out of sight while he waited for the right moment.

The tanks on both sides of the park stood their ground. The men inside trembled at the sight of Smitty's dragon, but they were trained to fight through their fear. All four tanks, two on each side, raised the long barrels of their cannons. Christian could hear clicking and clanging from inside them as the soldiers reloaded. Christian covered his ears just in time.

BOOM!

The screech from the dragon was deafening. Christian thought that perhaps the Army had won the day and peeked over the concrete to see what had become of the black beast.

The dragon, still on all fours, was unharmed. The shells from the tanks had simply bounced off the black scales, leaving the dragon angrier than harmed. The dragon arched its neck back like a snake about to strike and gurgled for a moment. The crystalline horn on the dragon's head glowed like a red ember, and its eyes were fixed on the foremost tank on the east side of the park. Its long neck stretched out quickly and its jaws opened wide, spilling out two columns of red and black flame that twirled around each other. The shadowy flames engulfed the tank, melting the armor, gun, and the soldiers inside. When the dragon stopped, all that remained was a black smoking mound of melted steel. The treads of the tanks had sunken into the melted asphalt.

BOOM!

It was all they could think of to do. The soldiers had reloaded and fired on the beast again. Christian wasn't ready for the second blast and could hear nothing but a loud, low tone ringing in his ears. It was like the sound of a deep windpipe when a gust of wind catches it but doesn't stop.

The dragon screamed in anger again and went on to the next tank. As it thrust its neck forward and spewed flame at the second tank on the east, Christian saw his chance. He dashed to the west side of the park. He crossed the street right in plain sight of the front tank. He saw the hatch on top pop open and a soldier stood and waved at him. Christian couldn't hear anything, but it was obvious that the Army man wanted him to get in the tank for safety. *That's the last place I want to be,* he thought and kept running.

He raced up the steps of the school and flung the doors open. It took him exactly thirty seconds to get to the top of the third floor. His heart beat in his chest against his ribs. He didn't know if it was from fear, or from sprinting up the steps. He burst through the door that led to the roof. The big sign on the front read "NO ACCESS - Official Use Only," but every kid at school had snuck up onto the roof at some point. Christian had done it on a dare. A double-dog dare, actually.

He ran to the edge of the roof to see the battle below in the park. It was going as he expected. The dragon had melted two tanks on the east and was now roasting the tank directly in front of the school… the one he decided not to climb into. *That poor soldier!*

The dragon had just started belching his black and red fire at the tank. His long neck stretched out parallel to the ground. *Not yet,* Christian told himself.

BOOM!

The fourth and last tank fired at the dragon while it was still working number three into a pile of molten goo. *Not yet… wait for it,* he told himself again.

The blast from the tank was enough to get the dragon's attention. The flames stopped, and the angry beast used its front clawed arm to flip the smoldering mass of the third tank upside down. When it turned towards the last armed enemy, it moved its body close to the school. The moment to act approached. *Only a couple more seconds.*

The dragon's neck arched back like a snake once again. The massive head raised up just feet away from the edge of the roof. It was now or never.

Christian took a breath and leapt off the edge of the roof, arms stretched out reaching for anything it could grab. He landed on the scaly neck and slid downwards towards its back. The beast shrieked in surprise and forgot all about the tank. It stumbled backwards and sideways. It reared up on its hind legs, then crashed down to shake off the unwelcomed rider.

But luck was with Christian and he held on.

The dragon swung his neck wildly from side to side. He thrashed left to right, then right to left. But Christian held on tight. He wrapped his arms and legs around the thick scaly neck of the black beast.

The dragon's screeching was terrible. The air and ground shook with every roar. Flame spewed from its mouth as it panicked and roared at the tiny rider. The park was on fire, as were the buildings surrounding it.

Christian knew he couldn't let this go on much longer. The fury of the dragon would burn the whole city to the ground. Also, his arms and legs would eventually be too tired to hang on. So he climbed. He would move one hand, grab a scale, then move his other hand up. Then he'd pull himself up a foot or so along the dragon's neck. Then he'd gripped the neck with his legs as his hand searched for the next scale. Higher and higher up the dragon's neck he climbed. The thrashing became worse and Christian found it much more difficult to hang on.

Hoops was in the alley, watching the spectacle from behind a dumpster. Toby and Eli watched as well, and all three boys feared they would watch Christian either be flung from the neck of the dragon and fall to his death or be eaten alive. The dragon was an invincible killer, too large for even the Army's tanks. What could one little boy with a knife do?

Christian didn't let go. He wouldn't quit climbing, either. The harder and harder the dragon flung his neck back and forth, the angrier and angrier Christian became. And his anger gave him strength. Finally, Christian reached the top of the dragon's neck. He waited for the beast to thrash its head downward. When the moment came, he slid down the long forehead of the dragon and grabbed the red crystal horn with both hands. It glowed like an ember and was almost as hot.

Christian knew he couldn't hold on to the fiery horn for long, so he let go with one hand, and held on to the horn with the other. He slipped his free hand around the white-bone handle of Hoops' magic knife and slid it from its sheath. With his eyes closed, he swung the blade upwards and struck the base of the horn, where it joined the nose of the dragon. When the edge of the blade touched the crystal, sparks spat out in all directions and the dragon screamed in pain. But it wasn't really the sound of a monstrous beast screeching in pain. It was more like the cry of a teenage boy.

Christian fell through the air. The blue-steeled knife in one hand, and the severed red crystal horn in his other hand. The enormous dragon very suddenly evaporated into black smoke that swirled into a tornado, just as it had when it first appeared. As Christian fell, he was caught in the rushing winds of the twister and saved from falling to his death on the ground below.

The black twister grew smaller and smaller. Within a few seconds, the shadowy smoke was gone and all that remained was Christian lying flat on top of a sleeping redheaded teenager in a red cloak.

When he realized he wasn't dead, Christian jumped to his feet and ran off towards the alley. Smitty lay unconscious on the ground in his red cloak, but his two shadows were very much awake. They dashed across the park after Christian. They crawled along the ground like snakes and were catching up to him.

"Hoops!" Christian yelled as loud as he could.

Hoops hopped out from behind the dumpster. "Over here!"

Just as the shadow wizards reached out and grabbed Christian's leg, he threw the red crystal wand across the street. It spun in the air and glowed like a red neon torch. Hoops judged where the crystal would land and sprinted towards it. He had to dive forward to catch it before it hit the ground and shattered. And in one smooth movement, Hoops caught the crystal wand with one hand, and rolled forward in a somersault. With his free arm, he snatched the timepiece from his pocket. It was already set to seven o'clock and wound tight. As the shadow wizards crawled across the street towards him, he gave the lid of the pocket watch a firm rubbing.

Whoosh.

The Oracle Quest

Hoops could only see the ground at his feet. It was washed in red light from the wand in his hand. The rest of the world was pitch black. No stars above could be seen. There was no horizon. While Hoops knew that Torpil was full of crystal fruit trees and luminous flowers, none could be seen.

He didn't know exactly where he was, but because he had used the timepiece to get there, he knew he wasn't in the bog. And probably he was close to the foot of the Oracle's mountain. That's where he appeared the last time he had used the timepiece to get to Torpil. But he couldn't be sure.

The canyon! Maybe the canyon can help me again!

He took a deep breath and yelled as loud as he could, "WHERE IS THE ORACLE!"

There was no echo and the sound of his voice went no farther than the wall of darkness surrounding him. It was like yelling into a pillow. The black air around him was thick, trapping any sound. The only thing Hoops could hear was the dirt under his sneakers as he shuffled around in the dark, looking for any ground that might seem familiar.

Suddenly, an icy breeze moved across his left ear and a man's voice whispered, "Go back. You must go back."

Across his right ear, he felt the icy breath of another voice whispering, "You hold the wand. You hold the power."

Malek and Trollkarl! The shadow wizards had followed him to Torpil. And now he was lost in the dark with those menacing wizards. Hoops was so frightened he couldn't think of anything to do but hide. He flung the hood over his head and squatted on the ground. But much to his surprise, when he was invisible, he could see the world around him! There was no color and it was still terribly dark, but he could see the world in black and white. It was like watching an old black and white movie while wearing sunglasses. He spun around to look at Malek and Trollkarl, but they were still invisible to him.

Hoops decided it was best to get moving and not wait around for the shadow wizards to appear. A quick look around told him he was in the clearing between the mountain and the canyon. Hoops saw the bottom of the path that zigzagged up the face of the Oracle's mountain and ran. There was no time to lose. Not only did Hoops feel like this mission needed to be completed as quickly as possible to save his friends, but he didn't want to spend any more time in the dark with Malek and Trollkarl.

As Hooped hurried up the stone steps along the path, he stayed ready to catch his balance if the ground quaked. But he was halfway up the mountain and there hadn't been a single rumble.

"Go back," the voice whispered in his left ear again. "We belong to you now.'

In his right ear, he felt the raspy breath saying, "With all the power... you can rule. With all the riches, you can save your friends."

"Shut up!" Hoops screamed at the voices. He defiantly stomped forward up the path.

"You can save your friends..." whispered Malek.

"You can bring Dewin back..." whispered Trollkarl.

Hoops paused for a moment. Rescuing Dewin was an impossibility. He was just an old, gnarly tree now. Surely, no magic could restore him.

"You can save Dewin..." both voices hissed. "Go back, Worthington. Don't do this."

****

The bleating of goats and sheep were the only sounds in the park. The smoldering tanks were still ablaze and made the air feel thick and hot. The stink of sulfur clung to everything. The park itself was torn to pieces. It was a chaotic mess of torn earth and scattered chunks of broken concrete. There was twisted metal and melted plastic where the playground used to be. Many of the park's trees had been ripped from the ground and laid on their sides, showing their roots.

On the edge of the park lay an unconscious redheaded teen, covered by a red cloak. Christian scampered by the boy. His four hooves click-clacked on the pavement as he hurried to the alley where his friends were. He had successfully tossed the red wand to Hoops but didn't escape the shadow wizards' wrath.

"MEH!" Christian bleated into the alley, but there was no reply. "MEH!" he yelled again, but his friends, hidden behind the dumpster, didn't move. Christian trotted into the alley and found Toby and Eli sitting side by side, with their backs against a brick wall. Their faces were covered in dirt and smudges of soot.

Toby looked at the goat and said to Eli, "Which traveler do you think this one is?"

Eli leaned forward and stroked Christian's neck and patted his white hairy shoulder. When he saw the loose leather belt dangling around the goat's bony hips, he cried, "It's Christian!"

"Poor Christian!" Toby leaned forward and hugged his friend.

Christian didn't care for the petting and hugging and pulled away. He walked to the mouth of the alley and bleated at Toby.

Eli said, "I think he wants you to follow him, Captain."

Toby got to his feet and followed Christian out of the alley. The white goat crossed the street, stopping only to turn and bleat again at Toby, who continued to follow. They stepped around fallen trees and hopped over holes in the asphalt. They passed burning tanks and a host of noisy, confused animals.

Christian stopped when he reached Smitty, who lay on the ground under his cloak. Toby was filled with rage at the sight of the redheaded brat. He ran full force to his sprawled-out body and kicked him in the ribs as hard as he could. But Smitty's body was under the red cloak and felt no pain. Smitty only opened his eyes and slowly began to stand. Toby kicked again as Smitty was on one knee, but the cloak protected him from any impact.

Smitty shouted for Malek and Trollkarl, but they never came. He kept his eyes on Toby, who burned with anger, ready for a fight, and walked backwards into the park. Several times, he tripped over broken concrete but got to his feet before Toby could jump on him.

Smitty retreated all the back way to what used to be the playground. Once again, he tripped, this time on the twisted, blackened chain that used to be part of the swing set. When he jumped back up to his feet, Christian trotted in close and grabbed the corner of the red cloak with his teeth.

"Let go, you little jerk!" Smitty screamed. But the little white goat wouldn't let go.

Toby lurched at Smitty, grabbed him by the hair, and yanked the red cloak off his shoulders. The fight was on.

****

"You can save your friends. You can restore your world," Malek hissed again.

"Don't do this, Worthington. You have the power to change everything," Trollkarl whined.

Hoops wanted to believe them. There was nothing he wanted more than to save Dewin and restore the Traveler's League. It was tempting. With the red wand, he could reverse all the damage that Smitty had unleashed in the Four Gates and Five Worlds. But he remembered Sentinel's warning, the great minotaur that guarded the Chamber of Crossroads, that the wizards must not escape. They must not have their way. Dewin had also warned Hoops they were dangerous.

"Shut up!" he cried at the shadow wizards. "Stop talking. It's over!"

Up and up he climbed, in the dark, with the glowing red wand in his hand. It became heavier and heavier with every step. When Hoops reached the cave that passed through the tip of the mountain, he had to rest. His knee was on fire. The sprain he had suffered in the park was getting worse, and he needed a few moments to rest before limping the rest of the way to the Oracle.

"You don't have to do this. Please!" Malek begged.

"Restore the light of Skuggi. All will be well. You can rule with your friends. You will be rich beyond your wildest dreams," Trollkarl pleaded.

The thoughts of wealth and power made Hoops daydream about a better life. He would have the admiration of the world, as a ruler. He would have the freedom to go on any adventure he wished, as a wealthy kid. He could save his friends and rebuild Traveler's Rest. They were tempting thoughts, but something about it still didn't feel right. The thought of taking the red wand for himself made him feel a little sick inside. For some reason, he couldn't quite remember, dropping the red wand into the Oracle's well was the right thing to do.

"Didn't I tell you to *shut up?!*?" Hoops barked at the voices in his ears. His flash of anger empowered him to keep going, so he limped to the other end of the cave and onto the path that wound around the top of the mountain.

But the voices didn't shut up.

"You're running out of time, Worthington. You must stop this nonsense!" Malek ordered.

"You're throwing away your future, boy," warned Trollkarl.

Hoops reached the shallow crater of the mountaintop. It was as quiet and gray as an old graveyard. When he saw the Oracle's well in its center, he felt as if it were miles away. Every step was labored and difficult. He felt like he was in a dream, one of those when he'd try to run away from something terrible, but his feet were slowed down by knee-deep mud. And with every heavy, slow step, the wizards begged, and pleaded, and tempted him.

"You could be the next captain!"

"You can save Green Dewin!"

"You can save the girl and her dwarf!"

"Think about your friends in Sirihbaz! You could rebuild their village."

"You could put an end to hate and violence of your city!"

Hoops wanted every one of those things to happen, but he still trudged on towards the well. He no longer had the strength to argue with the voices. He could no longer tell them to stop talking. His mind was weak. They were right, after all. He *could* set everything right and restore what Smitty had destroyed.

Hoops stood at the edge of the well. The voices no longer whispered. They screamed in his ears. They begged, as if for their very lives. Hoops raised the red glowing crystal wand over the gaping black mouth of the well. But his fingers were like stone. He tried to let go, but they wouldn't move.

"Please don't do this to us. We only want to restore our world. You'll kill us. We only want peace," Malek pleaded.

"Peace?" Hoops mumbled. He hadn't thought of that. Peace sounded really nice. It sounded like the solution to everything. "But there can't be peace if one person has all the power, I thought."

"You're wrong, Hoops," Trollkarl advised warmly. "One ruler is all it takes to secure peace in all of the worlds. You could save everybody and keep everyone... at peace." Trollkarl's voice was different, and familiar... "Think of your mother. Think of what you could do for her. She wouldn't have to work anymore..." It was the voice of his father! Hoops never talked about his dad, or the accident that took his life years ago. But the sound of his voice made Hoops cry. He missed him so much.

"Yes... think of your mother, Hoops."

Hoops tried one last time to release his grip of the wand. But the thought of his family was too powerful. His fingers wouldn't budge. *I can't do this. My mom. She needs me. This is my one chance to make things right for her. I have the power now to make things right... for Mom.*

"Yesssss..." the voices hissed in unison.

Suddenly, Hoops' cloak fluttered. From within a pocket, hidden in the folds of the cloth, King Tut scrambled out. He clawed his way up Hoop's shirt and onto his outstretched arm. The arm was as stiff as a tree branch, and the hand around the wand was locked tight. Though Hoops was powerless to move or release his grip, his eyes followed the mouse. King Tut carefully stepped onto the fist that held the wand. He turned to look at his master, who was unable to go any further.

"SQUEAK!" King Tut bared his little rodent teeth and bit into the soft flesh of Hoops' hand between the knuckles of his thumb and forefinger.

"OUCH!" cried Hoops as he yanked his hand back from the well, releasing his grip. Both the wand and the mouse tumbled into the blackness of the Oracle's well.

The Balance is Restored

Anger fueled Toby who didn't let up his assault on Smitty. He had landed several good punches. Toby was only a year older but was definitely bigger. His body had already begun to transform from a boy's scrawny and bony physique, to the muscular frame of a man. Smitty wasn't quite as developed. But while Toby was stronger, Smitty was definitely quicker, and more cunning. He was, after all, the fox.

Toby did well to stand between Smitty and the red cloak that laid on the ground. Without it, its magic armor couldn't protect Smitty. The fox made several attempts to get past Toby and snatch the cloak, but Toby landed a few punches on Smitty's face and put an end to that strategy. Enraged, Smitty picked up a twisted metal bar. It was a monkey bar from the playground that had been torn off and burnt black by the dragon. Smitty had the advantage with this weapon. Before Toby could find something useful to fight back with, Smitty struck him in the sides of his knees. Toby winced in pain and was off balance for a moment. And a moment was all Smitty needed. Another swing at Toby's head knocked him to the ground. He had raised his arms to block the bar just in time, but the blow was enough to send him into the dirt.

Smitty jumped on his fallen enemy and wrapped his hands around Toby's throat. He squeezed while Toby tried to pry his fingers away.

Toby's legs kicked as he struggled unsuccessfully to get Smitty off him. He couldn't get free, couldn't breathe, and wondered if this was the end.

Tighter and tighter, Smitty squeezed. Toby just couldn't get out from under him, nor could he pry away his fingers. Toby's vision blurred and darkened. Just as he was about to black out, he saw Eli standing behind Smitty with a chunk of broken concrete in his hand.

Whack!

With one hit, Eli knocked Smitty to the ground. The redhead fell sideways like a tree and was out cold.

As the Keeper knelt down and kept watch over Smitty's unconscious body, whooshing sounds were heard all over the park. The hundreds of animals all started crying, baaing, mooing, oinking, and barking. But one by one, their voices were cut off by a peculiar whooshing sound. Toby looked away from Eli and Smitty to see what was happening... all of the animals were transforming back into boys! Aiden appeared near the playground. Gavin was near the fountain. Eva Mae appeared across the street, and all of the boys of the Traveler's League throughout the park! In addition to the boys, and much to Toby's surprise, WolliPogs appeared. All of the sheep that had flooded the city streets changed back into the WolliPogs who had once been enslaved by Braxo, then transformed by Smitty.

Toby realized that the magic of the red wand was being reversed. He yelled at Eli, "It worked! Eli, look! It worked! He did it! Hoops did it! We're saved!"

Eli rose to his feet, and looked around. He and Toby joyfully laughed together as they watched all of their friends restored.

Not only were the boys, friends, and WolliPogs restored, but the mirrors of the six-thirty world were no longer clouded. And the blankets of darkness that encased the five worlds, stealing their light, evaporated. The dragon's venomous clouds of black fire and smoke were torn away from the skies and the sun shined again.

"Hey, guys! You mind if I keep this cloak?"

Toby and Eli turned towards the voice behind them to find Christian, restored to his handsome boy body. He still wore Hoops' belt and had recovered his bone-handled knife. He held the fox's red cloak in his hands and smiled like a pirate that accidentally found a chest full of gold doubloons!

Toby and Eli laughed and greeted their friend with a hug. They recounted each other's brave deeds excitedly and talked about rebuilding Traveler's Rest and restoring the League. A familiar whooshing sound interrupted them. Behind them, a swirl of yellow magic particles flashed, and Hoops appeared. His shoulders drooped under his cloak and his cheeks were marked by tears that had streaked down the dirt on his face.

His friends welcomed him warmly and congratulated him on a job well done. But Hoops couldn't share their joy. He had lost his *best* friend. King Tut had fallen into the well. And while the Oracle was able to restore light to the worlds, imprison the shadow wizards, and restore his friends, it all came at a cost. And the cost of losing his little mouse dampened the sweetness of victory, and the joy of being saved.

"Cheer up, Hoops," Toby said. "Everything has been set back to normal. Perhaps Tut is alive somewhere! Maybe he's in Torpil and you just didn't find him before coming back."

Hoops hoped that Toby was right about that, but it didn't make him feel much better, thinking his little buddy was alone in some strange world with no one to care for him. He said nothing in return. He simply walked home, with tears once again coming to his eyes. A flicker of anger in his heart made him pull the cloak off his shoulders, wad it up into a big ball, and throw it to the ground.

"Squeak!" said the cloak.

Hoops stopped when he heard the sound and watched. The folds of the cloak twisted, jiggled, and fluttered with movement as his majesty, King Tut, found his way out from underneath it. Hoops scooped him up and held him close with his heart full of relief and gratitude. He ran back to his friends in the park to show them the good news. But when he found them, they stood in a circle with worried looks on their faces. They were no longer celebrating.

Hoops pushed his way into the circle and stood next to Eva Mae, who hugged him immediately. She and GeriPog had found the boys in the center of the park, as did many of the restored travelers.

"What's going on, Toby?" Hoops asked. "Why does everyone look so worried? What's wrong? We won. We fixed everything! Right?"

Toby glanced briefly at Christian, then back to Hoops. "Smitty got away again... snuck off somehow; I guess while we were celebrating. He's gone."

The End

Note from the Author

NICHOLAS GOSS has been a piano teacher, sailboat builder, private investigator, barista, and salesman. He has a collection of more books than he could possible read in his lifetime and lives with his head firmly stuck in the clouds. He resides in Nashville with his wife, two kids, and their labradoodle, Shelby. His host of eccentric hobbies include woodworking, sailing, fencing, ping pong, hammocking, and playing the penny whistle. Can you imagine what his neighbors must think?

Yeah. You guessed it: he was homeschooled.

The Traveler's League Book Series was born when he strayed from the normal bedtime routine of reading, and instead created new worlds full of funny characters, action, magic, and adventure. Since then, he has committed himself to entertaining children through writing books that make kids feel the magic of adventure and friendship. All the books in the series are available on Amazon.

Made in the USA
Coppell, TX
28 May 2020

26622747R00116